CATHERINE MacPHAIL

NEMESIS
RIDE OF DEATH

JF

BLOOMSBURY
LONDON BERLIN NEW YORK

To Emma and Helen

First published in Great Britain in 2008 by Bloomsbury Publishing Plc
36 Soho Square, London, W1D 3QY

A CIP catalogue record of this book is available from the British Library

ISBN 978 0 7475 8271 7

All papers used by Bloomsbury Publishing are natural, recyclable products made
from wood grown in well-managed forests. The manufacturing processes conform
to the environmental regulations of the country of origin.

Typeset by Dorchester Typesetting Group Ltd
Printed in Great Britain by Clays Ltd, St Ives Plc

3 5 7 9 10 8 6 4 2

www.macphailbooks.com
www.bloomsbury.com

FSC
Mixed Sources
Product group from well-managed
forests and other controlled sources
Cert no. SGS-COC-2061
www.fsc.org
© 1996 Forest Stewardship Council

The paper this book is printed on is certified independently in accordance with the rules of the FSC.

It is ancient-forest friendly. The printer holds chain of custody.

00

SUNDAY 1.15 A.M.

Dead of night. Something woke me. It took me a moment to remember where I was – to shake the memories of the past few days back into my head. Was it only yesterday that I had escaped the Dark Man again, vowing that from then on *I* would follow *him*?

So, where are you now, Ram? I asked myself.

I remembered his car had come up behind the farm truck I had escaped in. I knew he would be after me, would be close behind me. And sure enough, I hadn't had to wait long. There he was. I saw his face behind the wheel of the car. He looked furious. Had I something to do with that anger? I hoped so. I had stayed out of his clutches yet again.

But he had surprised me. Instead of following the main road, he had turned on to a slip road. Not after me at all. Going somewhere else . . . but where? And why?

That was when I had jumped from the truck and rolled on to the grass verge. The wet road made it easy to follow the tyre tracks. Where could he be heading, I wondered, down that quiet side road?

I had walked, it seemed, for ages. Dark morning became even darker afternoon, and finally I could no longer make out his tracks. They were lost among those of tractors and lorries and other cars. Where had he gone from there? Was it a shortcut? But a shortcut to where?

I had kept walking, my eyes scanning the road for any sign of him. It was the icy rain and the darkness that had finally stopped me. I had found shelter in this old deserted church. Outlined against the fast-moving clouds, gargoyles of mythical creatures, their faces ugly and stark, seemed to leap from every turret. Not a comforting place to rest – and it had no roof. But at least there were lots of nooks and crannies and alcoves out of the rain and wind where I could hide myself away and figure out my next move.

I wasn't worried about losing the Dark Man. I knew the best way to find him was to let *him* find *me*.

My clothes had dried into my skin, cold and stiff. I curled myself into a ball, rubbed at my arms. I longed to be warm. I was so hungry that if I'd seen a bird scrabbling for a worm, it might have had to fight me for it.

I hadn't meant to sleep. But after what I had been through, who could blame me?

There was a sound. An owl hooting? And then a bird flapped across the night sky. I was convinced that one of those gargoyles' horned heads turned to watch it. The jitters were definitely getting to me. Perhaps, I thought, I could find somewhere not so isolated, closer to a town, to spend the rest of the night.

I sat up and looked round. It was dark, but winter

nights in those parts were dark for so long. There was hardly any daylight. It had stopped raining but the sky was still thick with clouds. If there was a moon, it was well hidden. I even thought of lying back down again, going back to sleep till morning.

But I had no time to waste.

'Time is running out.'

The words repeated themselves in my head. I didn't understand. I only knew it was a fact. That was about the only thing I did know. Even my name was a mystery. I called myself Ram and didn't know why, just knew it was important – no random choice.

I stood up and brushed myself down, wrapped my arms about me to try to keep warm. I stumbled out of the church, tripping over the flagstones on the ground – no, not flagstones. I stepped back quickly. These were gravestones. I was walking over the graves of people from an ancient past. Definitely time to move on.

I came out of the church, tried to remember how I'd got there. I had left the road and crossed a field, then climbed over a broken wall. Now all I wanted was to find my way to the road again. As I walked, my eyes peered through the dark, to the left and to the right, looking for a path, for a sign that would lead me out.

Too bad I wasn't looking down. One minute I was walking on solid ground and the next I was falling, my arms flailing in mid-air. I didn't make a sound – didn't have time. I crashed face down, landing hard.

I was on my feet in an instant. Where was I? I saw only darkness. My face ached with pain. I began to feel my way around. My hands touched earth. I spread out my fingers, moving them along one wall till they could go no further, turning along a shorter wall, then turning again, and then again – back to where I had started.

Two long sides, with two shorter sides at each end. Man-made, that was for certain. Not a square . . . What did you call a shape like that? An oblong? The word came to me from somewhere. I had fallen into an oblong hole, almost like a box – long enough to lie down in.

My teeth began to chatter, and it was nothing to do with my frozen clothes. It was as if iced water was being poured down my back. My whole body started to shake.

Because in that second, I knew exactly where I was.

I had fallen into an open grave.

01

I leapt as high as I was able, desperately trying to grasp a hold in the hard earth. The clouds parted briefly, teasing me with enough light to see how deep I had fallen. Then it was all darkness again. There was the eerie sound of that distant owl – my only company. At least, I *hoped* it was my only company. I tried to dig my fingers into the earth, but they could get a grip of nothing.

I wanted to yell out. Yet I was afraid. Afraid of what might be lurking out there in the dark. Maybe not just an owl.

I made as much of a run as I could and jumped again . . . but I was in too deep.

How deep was I?

Six feet under.

Something in my hidden past told me that.

I wouldn't panic. I would not panic!

Think rationally, Ram. This was a freshly dug grave. Even if I had to stay there all night, someone would surely be around in the morning.

Spend a night in an open grave?

Not on your nelly! I would get out of there. I'd find a

way. But how? There was nothing to stand on, no room for me to make a leap and nothing to hold on to if I could. No handy foothold. Nothing.

I took a deep breath, tried to calm my rattling nerves. OK, if there was no foothold, I would make one. I frantically dug my fingers into the sides until I was sure they must be bleeding. It was March; the earth this deep was still concrete hard. But I was terrified of being down there and that terror turned my fingers into steel claws. The blood pumped through my head as if it would come bursting out of my ears at any second. I clawed at the side, kicked it. The slightest dent would give me hope.

Why were these things always happening to me? Wasn't I in enough trouble?

And only days left. Time running out. I had something to do, something to stop. I had to have stayed alive for a reason. It wasn't the first time I'd thought that.

I would get out of there.

I had to . . .

How long it took I don't know, but at last! I could bury my fingers into one tiny little hole in the earth. It was all I had made, but it gave me hope, and a start. I sunk my fingertips in as deep as I could and hauled myself higher. Centimetres higher. But when I dug my fingers in the earth above, some soil came loose. I made a desperate grab for the next hold, terrified I would lose my grip and fall again. I clung on, willing myself to move. I had to get out, one foothold at a time, one finger hold at a time.

It seemed to take for ever. I used the groove I had

2

made below for a foothold while I dug above me with my fingers. My arms cried with pain. My fingers were almost numb. Yet still I climbed.

When my hand touched the grass at the top I gripped it, held on fast. Wet with icy dew, it began to slip through my fingers. I had visions of myself tumbling into that black pit again. No way. I couldn't bear the thought of that. Above me, a hand's length away, there was a young tree. I lunged at it. The bark cut into my fingers, but I would not let go, and started to haul myself to the top.

I was almost out.

I clung there for a moment, half in, half out, gasping for breath. My legs still dangled inside the grave. Then my imagination brought skeletal hands up from below, rising out of the earth, reaching to drag me down again. With a split-second movement I pulled myself higher, swung my legs up and over on to the grass and rolled away from that open grave. As I did, my jacket caught on the sharp little branches of the tree. I almost let out a cry, because for a moment I was sure the tree had come alive, and was reaching for me with gnarled bony fingers, to throw me back down. My jacket ripped as I yanked it free, part of the sleeve fluttering on one of the branches. I scrabbled away from it, away from the grave; tried to get my breath back.

Only then did I sit up and look around me. My eyes were more accustomed to the dark now and I could see the outlines of gravestones in all directions, surrounding the church. I leant back to rest, whipped round when I realised what I was leaning against. One of those old gravestones. The inscription was so worn I could hardly read it.

OWEN BALFOUR
1891–1923
DEATH MAY SOON CALL YOU

02

That really gave me the creeps. It was like some kind of warning.

Death may soon call you. Nice thought, Owen.

1923 – that was almost a century ago. This graveyard was as deserted as the church, overgrown, filled with broken gravestones, overflowing with the dead.

My eyes went back to the open grave yawning in front of me. Well, someone new was moving in. I got to my feet. That was the explanation, no mystery here. There must be a funeral tomorrow. A freshly dug grave waiting for a new tenant . . . and it had almost been me. I only wanted away from that place. I began to hurry, my eyes on the ground now, just in case. I had no intention of falling into another grave.

I was so intent on watching the ground, trying to find the path, that I might have walked into her . . . or through her.

But something made me look up. Some movement out of the corner of my eye.

She was heading towards me through the darkness, the figure of a girl – the cold breeze billowing her white dress around her.

5

I couldn't see her eyes.

Did she have eyes?

She was stumbling, her arms outstretched, her long black hair falling over her face, hiding her features.

She didn't look real.

I wanted to scream. I tried to scream, but it wouldn't come. The vision was terrifying, advancing through the dark trees and the gravestones. It was as if my throat was closing up so tight that no sound could pass through. Had I seen her before? I felt I had – somewhere in that nightmare past.

I took a step back. She still came, moving closer, not making a sound. Silent as death.

As death.

Was she the angel of death, coming for me? I'd been certain I'd been kept alive for a reason, but maybe it just hadn't been my time to die. Not then.

But maybe now, tonight, in this lonely graveyard. Now . . . it *was* my turn.

She was reaching out to me. I had a feeling that when she looked up and I saw those eyes, it would be the end for me. There would be no escape. I imagined her touching me, her fingers snatching at my clothes, clutching me to her, and then it would all be over.

NO!

That's when I moved. No. No end for me. No way. I was going to live.

I turned away from her and ran. I tried not to think of her behind me. In my imagination she began to fly, was suddenly above me. It was so clear in my mind I even looked up, took my eyes off the path for a second and went tumbling to the ground. I was on my feet in the same instant, still running. Ahead of me I could make out the cemetery gates.

They only added to the nightmare. The gates were locked tight. Heavy iron chains with padlocks wound round the railings. Snakes and skulls intertwined with the iron like a vision from hell. I shook those gates, rattled them, dared a look back. She was still there. It seemed to me she floated closer. I put my foot into the mouth of a skeleton and began to climb. My fingers closed round a serpent's tail and I pulled myself higher. My foot slipped, but I clung on, trying not to think of what was behind me. I just kept climbing and, reaching the top at last, swung myself over and jumped – didn't even think of the height.

I hit the ground hard. And I ran. I ran till I could hardly breathe. I ran even when I had no more breath. Still I ran. I ran back on to the road. Only then did I turn to look, sure I would see her.

But she was gone.

And even then, I didn't stop running.

03

I was shaking with terror as I ran. What was it I had seen? A ghost? One of the undead? A *zombie*? The word came to me. A zombie – a creature who comes alive after death and eats human flesh. I almost fell, I stopped running so suddenly. There was a picture in my head . . . a movie in a dark theatre – no, not a theatre, a house, *my* house. A zombie movie . . . laughing, shrieking, throwing popcorn – trying to hide the terror I felt as the creatures lurched towards some hapless victim.

'*He's too young to watch that!*' a woman's voice called out. Not angry, laughing too. My *mother*? Was I remembering the voice of my mother?

The image was gone in an instant. Why couldn't I hold on to my memories? Yet the terrifying vision I had seen had brought something back to me. And it occurred to me that it was always fear that made me remember. If only I could piece these threads of memory together, hold them for longer than a few seconds.

I bent over, my hands on my knees, trying to get my breath back. I dared to turn and look again. There was only black road behind me. The figure was gone. Had I really seen something? I started to doubt it. It couldn't have been real, had to have been my imagination. I had fallen into a grave. Of course my mind would be playing tricks on me.

I pictured again that piece of my jacket fluttering on the branch of the tree, and her dress, too, fluttering in the night breeze. It must have been my imagination, I thought, because I definitely didn't believe in ghosts. But I had had enough of the dark. I wasn't going to risk my imagination going into overdrive again. I ran on to find life, and lights, and people.

I was desperate to be out of the dark.

'Gallacher's dead, thanks to that boy!'

His associates were angry. He didn't tell them that it was, in fact, thanks to him that Gallacher was dead. He'd held out a hand to save his friend, his colleague for so many years, and at the last moment he had saved the boy instead. Not a wise thing to admit to his associates.

The boy would die – he wanted to assure them of that – but only when he, the Dark Man, was ready.

'He's not immortal,' he told them. *But he is special*, he wanted to add. He had always known the boy was special.

'We have no more time to waste on this,' was their answer. 'Find him, and kill him.'

It was a pile of newspapers smacking down on the pavement that woke me up. I had found the doorway of a corner shop to sleep in. I lay still, hardly breathing, curled up in the corner, not wanting anyone to know I was there. I had discovered it was safer that way. The van hadn't even stopped, only slowed down to dump its load. It roared away, too loud in the early morning silence. It was still dark, but there was just a hint of light on the horizon. I shivered with cold, pulled my stiff jacket tighter around me. Soon this little corner shop would open. I would have to move on, find somewhere else. But for the moment the road was quiet and empty. I dragged the pile of newspapers towards me. I wanted to see what day it was, what date.

It was Sunday. These were the Sunday newspapers. They were tied up with string, but I could make out the headlines:

US PRESIDENT TO HEAD HOME TOMORROW

CONFERENCE ON TERRORISM DECLARED A SUCCESS

WORLD LEADERS UNITE TO FIGHT WORLD TERRORISM

And underneath, in smaller headlines:

POLITICIAN'S DAUGHTER STILL MISSING: TERRORISTS BLAMED

I slipped one of the papers out of the pile and curled back into the corner to read it.

But the story of this conference only held my interest for a second. It was the column on the side that really brought me awake:

Am I the only person left alive who believes the lone bomber wasn't alone?
Emir Khan on the conspiracy theory, page 3.

04

7 A.M.

Footsteps were coming along the lonely street. I cowered back and covered myself with the newspaper. I held my breath as they stopped right beside the doorway. Any second now I expected a long arm to reach out and grab me. A gruff policeman moving me on, or worse, asking questions I couldn't answer.

I needn't have worried. Whoever it was either didn't notice me or didn't care. A paper was tugged from the pile, and I heard some change being thrown on top for payment.

It made me smile. Even here, on a quiet street, when it would be so easy to steal, decent people never did.

I waited till the tattoo of footsteps had faded before I opened the paper at page three and began to read.

It was dark in the doorway and I had to peer at the words to see them:

Just a few weeks ago a bomb went off in London. We have been told the perpetrator, whom we have all come to call the 'Lone Bomber', was acting on his own. An ex-soldier, invalid-

ed out of the army and possibly suffering from Gulf War Syndrome, he became paranoid. He began to see conspiracies everywhere and was eventually forcibly retired from his civil service post. Even at the time, we have now been told, there were people who warned he might do something that would threaten the security of this country.

And it seemed their fears were justified. The bomb he planted could have killed hundreds, including the Prime Minister. But it went off early, and he was the only casualty.

At least, that's what we've been told.

But in the weeks since the bombing, many eye witnesses – people who were on the scene at the time – have died in what might be called 'mysterious circumstances'.

Brian Farrel, was the first: he suffered a heart attack while driving his taxi, killing him instantly. Farrel was only thirty-two years old and had no history of heart problems.

Joanna Impinenti, a fifty-year-old teacher, fell from the window of her fifth-floor flat. A tragic accident, was the official story.

Edward Moore, a traffic warden, was the victim of a hit and run. And only two days ago, Colin Drummond, a retired businessman, drowned in his own swimming pool.

No suspicious circumstances . . . except they were all eye witnesses to what happened that day.

I don't believe the Lone Bomber was working alone. I have never believed that. What if he were part of a bigger conspiracy?

Do you have any information that could help me? Or are you a witness, afraid to step forward?

Was that why the Dark Man was after me – I was an eye

witness, I had seen something that day? Did he plan to torture me or drug me till he found out what it was?

Well, I had plenty of information to give Emir Khan, didn't I? Information – and the photograph. The photograph of the Lone Bomber with Gallacher and the Dark Man. There was a number at the bottom of the article for people to call if they had information. I read the phone number again, memorised it.

I was disturbed by the sound of a car turning on to the dark road. It seemed to be slowing to a halt. The shopkeeper coming to open up maybe. There wasn't time to read any more. Could I call this Emir Khan, tell him what I knew? Phone calls cost money, I thought, and I had none. I clocked the coins lying on top of the pile of newspapers. It wouldn't really be stealing. I would make up for it . . . and it was for a worthy cause, wasn't it? I had no choice. I picked up a coin, enough for the call, and with a silent apology I slipped away from the doorway and hurried off down the street.

It was only when I rounded the corner, backed into an alleyway, that I realised how much I was shaking.

The Lone Bomber hadn't been working on his own. I knew that already. But now I knew I wasn't the only one who had discovered that. And one by one we were being killed off. Why?

Emir Khan suspected there was a conspiracy. He wanted to hear from anyone else. Here, at last, was someone I could surely trust, someone who would help me. I was going to call Emir Khan.

05

Emir Khan knew his story would rattle people. He already knew he was in danger because of what he believed. But it was a story that had to be told. He had to take the chance. Only yesterday, another witness had died. Colin Drummond had been a proficient swimmer who got into difficulties in his own pool. Cramp? Possibly. No suspicious circumstances, the police said.

No suspicious circumstances when the others had died either. All dead, all the witnesses he knew about. One by one they had been disposed of.

He, Emir Khan, had seen nothing, knew nothing. He had been nowhere near the scene at the time of the explosion – hadn't even been in London. He had no proof, just the gut instinct of a seasoned reporter that there was more to this story. The article was meant to bring another witness, silent till now, out of the woodwork. There had to be someone, somewhere, surely?

But he knew his article would be noticed by others too: the dangerous, shadowy men he believed were behind this conspiracy. And he was sure there was a conspiracy.

Jane Faulkner picked up the paper during her break at the hospital where she worked as a nurse. It had been a quiet night shift, and she was keen to read the latest in the story of the missing politician's daughter. A publicity stunt, the gossip columns had been saying. That's what many people thought. Angus Lennox was up for re-election and looking for the sympathy vote. His daughter, Sapphire, was a wild child, always being snapped by the paparazzi in one nightclub or another, always partying. She had a book coming out – ghost written no doubt. This would be her way of making sure it had the maximum publicity.

Yet, Jane wasn't so sure. A politician would surely never risk staging something like that. Lennox had looked genuinely distraught when she had seen him on television. He seemed to adore his daughter, in spite of her being a constant embarrassment to him. Didn't he have a pet name for her . . . What was it again? He had brought her up on his own after his wife's death. As to Sapphire, she was wild, yes – but she was young, she was pretty and she was spoiled. It had never seemed to Jane that she had any real badness in her. To let her father think his beloved daughter, his only child, had been kidnapped would be cruel in the extreme.

The Sunday paper put aside speculation about the publicity stunt though, and reported that some kind of terrorist organisation had claimed responsibility for the kidnapping. The paranoia about terrorism was intensifying. But it was a column at the side of the page that caught Jane's eye. She opened the paper at page three and read the article.

Emir Khan . . . Phone me if you have a story. And then the number.

She was fed up trying to tell her story. She'd told the police on the day of the bombing – told them what she'd seen. She'd been assured it was of no importance; nothing to do with the bombing. It had been filed away.

And they were probably right.

What she had seen was such a little thing.

It had niggled at her though. She'd heard stories too, about witnesses dying mysteriously. And she had begun to feel afraid.

Best keep your mouth shut, she'd decided. But she wasn't the kind of woman who liked keeping her mouth shut.

And now this. *Discretion guaranteed*, the article assured her. *If you have anything to tell, get in touch with me.* And that phone number.

What harm would it do to call? Perhaps she would do it just before she finished her shift.

The Dark Man saw the article too. Khan was a nuisance. He had wanted him out of the way from the beginning. He had warned his associates about him.

But they hadn't been concerned about Khan. The man knew nothing. His speculation had been dismissed as a reporter going for a story, or making one up if one wasn't there. He wasn't considered a danger.

This was different though. Now he was asking for

17

witnesses to come forward. Even though after tomorrow it wouldn't matter what Emir Khan or anyone else said, the Dark Man was going to suggest he should be disposed of – for good.

06

Emir Khan put the phone down. He'd had several calls, all from cranks. Some had been convinced they'd seen little green men that day. One had said he'd seen Elvis with a bomb hidden in his guitar case. And another claimed that he knew the Lone Bomber wasn't alone, because he'd marched into that underground car park along with the seven dwarves. Emir had begun to think that perhaps his colleagues back at the London office had been right. Giving the phone number of the flat – even though it belonged to the newspaper and wasn't his – was asking for trouble.

But then this last call, this one was genuine. Jane Faulkner. Had he heard the name before? He'd learned the names of almost all the 'conspiracy witnesses', as he called them. But the woman had said she'd only given the police one statement. Her story had been brushed aside, or 'under the carpet', as she put it.

Was she in any danger? That was the first thing she wanted to know. He had reassured her that he wouldn't reveal her identity in his story. She'd be safe.

Was that true, though? He hoped so. Too many had died already. He had made an arrangement to meet her at Waverley Station at ten o'clock, as soon as her shift finished. No time to waste. He'd been sent to Glasgow to cover the conference. He could drive to Edinburgh easily by ten.

He lifted the phone again, examined it. Was it tapped? Would he know if it was? Or was he becoming as paranoid as everyone said he was. He'd seen his colleagues raising their eyes at any mention he made of a conspiracy; he'd watched them avoiding him whenever he approached.

And then the phone rang again, its shrill tone cutting the air in his quiet flat.

He hoped it wasn't another crank call.

I had expected Emir Khan to sound Asian. He didn't. If anything, his accent was American. 'Emir Khan speaking. Do you have information for me?' That was the first thing he said. Straight to the point.

How could I begin? I didn't even know my name. So I jumped right into the part I did know. 'I have a photograph of the Lone Bomber.' I patted my pocket to reassure myself it was still there. 'He's with two men. They're both involved in the conspiracy.' I rattled on, eager to tell my story. 'And there *is* a conspiracy. They were both after me. One of them's dead now, but the other – he'll never give up till he gets me. I know something – something really important . . .' I hesitated, wishing I could tell him more. 'Trouble is, I don't know what it is. I've lost my memory.' I knew I was beginning to talk too fast. Excitement, fear, getting the better of me. 'There's something big coming. The bombing was just the beginning of it. If I could just remember . . .'

'Calm down.' His voice was soft. 'I'll help you; I'll find somewhere safe for you. I'm meeting another witness later. I can meet you too. I'll help you remember.' And I believed him. He would find a way to bring my memory back. I felt as if a curtain was about to be lifted from my past.

'Where are you phoning from?'

It had never occurred to me to check where I was, but I did now. I looked at the number on the phone, at the advertisements for local taxis and restaurants on the walls of the phone box. 'I think I'm in a place called Haddington.'

'Haddington! That's Edinburgh. Do you know where Waverley Station is? It's the main railway station in Edinburgh.'

'I'll find it,' I told him.

'I'm meeting a woman there this morning, at ten. Can you make that?'

'I'll be there. How will I know you?'

He paused to think about it. 'Tell you what, I'll wear a red baseball cap. You'll see me coming for miles.'

'And you'll know me,' I told him. 'I'll be the boy who looks lost.'

Emir put down the phone carefully, but his hand was shaking. He had struck gold, he was sure of it. A boy, who knew so much, who had a photograph.

A boy. He had once interviewed the Impinenti

woman, and she had mentioned a boy. Then she had died. Had any of the others seen a boy? But it couldn't be that same boy . . . could it?

What if it was? He hadn't even asked his name. He picked up a pen and, on the pad beside the phone, under *Jane Faulkner*, added: *The boy with no name. 10 a.m.*

He looked at his watch. Still early morning. Time for him to get what he needed together before he drove to Edinburgh to meet Jane Faulkner and the boy. The boy, especially, would have to be kept safe. Emir wondered where he could take him, who he could trust.

His thoughts were interrupted by a knock at the door. He was close to exposing the biggest story of his career. This boy could be the key. He wished now he had told him he would meet him right away, that he would drive to Haddington and pick him up. Never mind, not long to wait now. He walked to the door and opened it.

07

9.50 A.M.

After her shift was finished, Jane Faulkner came in on the train. She hated every minute of it. Usually she loved the ride into Waverley – that first sight of the castle looming above as the train emerged from the tunnel always took her breath away. That was really something.

But she didn't enjoy it today. The train was packed full, even at this hour on a Sunday. The peace marches planned for tomorrow, both here and in Glasgow, had brought people in their hordes. She had to stand all the way, and when the train stopped at her usual station, only streets from her home, she had to fight the urge to jump out and run. Why had she said she would meet this Emir Khan anyway? She could have been home soon, sipping her morning tea and, after church, looking forward to a lovely duvet day in bed. She could have gone home, kept her mouth shut and just got on with her life.

She was glad to step off the train at last, or, rather, be carried from it in the surge of people trying to get out. She wandered round to the main concourse and looked all around her. The news-stand was busy, but that was where Emir Khan had told her to wait. She wished she knew what he looked like. Was there anyone who looked as if they might be a journalist? Emir Khan. An Asian presumably. There was a multitude of Asian faces in the station, and white. She herself was black, second generation British.

She'd buy another newspaper, she decided. She might as well read more about the kidnapping. There had been a ransom demand. It was all the talk at the hospital, among staff and patients alike. Now that a terrorist organisation had claimed responsibility, everyone's opinion had changed. Something had to be done about terrorism, they were all saying. And then conversations would move on to the big conference of world leaders that was taking place that weekend. They had worked out a joint plan of action – at least that was the statement given to the press. But no one believed anything politicians said or did these days.

She paid for her paper and wandered round the stand, her eyes searching the station for someone who might be Emir Khan. There were so many entrances to Waverley, she didn't know which one to look at. There were businessmen and women hurrying to and from trains, carrying briefcases and laptops, speaking urgently on their mobile phones – working even on a Sunday. Mothers and fathers hurried by, pushing toddlers in strollers – families going on a day trip somewhere. Tourists stood around studying street maps; people carried banners and flags for the peace marches.

She saw a boy standing by the stairs – thin, wiry, with a mop of thick dark hair. He was scanning the crowds as intently as she was. She hoped he wasn't a beggar, but he didn't look like one. He looked as if he was waiting for someone too.

I was early. I watched the hands on the clock above the concourse as they clicked towards ten o'clock. I had been wandering round the station for what seemed like hours, until I saw a security man watching me suspiciously.

'No begging!' he called out.

Begging indeed! But I decided to keep out of his way. So I had taken a place in a doorway near the stairs. From there I could see people come and go, watch for Emir Khan and his red baseball cap.

A woman at the news-stand noticed me. I saw her eyes pass over me, then dart back and lock on to me.

Emir Khan had told me he was meeting someone else. Could this woman be that someone else? Her skin was black like chocolate, and she was wearing a nurse's uniform under her short jacket. Her eyes stayed on me for so long, I had to look away, and when I glanced back she was intent on the paper she was reading.

Right then my arm was gripped and my first reaction was to run, to kick out, till a voice said softly, 'Are you waiting for me? I'm Emir Khan.'

I turned and looked into a smiling Asian face, a man with deep brown eyes. 'You're the boy who called me?' he asked. I nodded at him.

'I want to get you out of here.' He looked at his watch. 'My car's parked round the corner. Come on.'

I didn't move. 'You said you were meeting someone else – a woman. Is she here yet?'

His eyes moved beyond me. 'Yeah, she's here. I'll come back in and fetch her. I just want you safe in the car for now.'

Jane couldn't concentrate on her paper. Something was niggling at her, something about the boy. She looked up again and caught a glimpse of him as he was climbing the stairs out of the station. He seemed to have found who he'd been waiting for. He was definitely with someone now.

Her foot tapped against something. She looked down. One of those businessmen had left his case beside the news-stand. It was tucked behind the counter, almost out of sight.

It was that *tucked* that worried her. Tucked. Hidden. Maybe not forgotten at all.

Nonsense. She would not be caught up in this paranoia that there were terrorists on every corner, in spite of having been so close to the London bombing herself. Nevertheless . . .

She stepped back from the case, looked around for the security guard, and spotted him disappearing behind one of the shopping booths. She began to hurry towards him.

08

10 A.M.

We were almost out of the station when the bomb exploded. It threw me off my feet. Emir Khan grabbed me by the shoulder – if it hadn't been for him, I would have smashed face down on the iron stairs. I'd never heard an explosion like it.

Yes, I had. A split second of a memory. Another place. Another bomb . . .

A split second of eerie silence after the explosion, and then all hell broke loose. The memory was swallowed by all the chaos and confusion around me.

Emir Khan was still on his feet. 'Come on, we have to get out of here.' He was pulling me away. I could hardly see him. He was a figure lost in smoke. I could hardly hear his voice above the screams.

I stood up, began to stumble after him. It was as if the station had been transported in a flash to another nightmare world. One second, people were hurrying about their business, the next, just as the clock clicked on to the hour, 10 a.m., their world crashed. I looked up to where that clock had been. It was gone now – there was

27

just an iron beam trembling on the roof of the station, held by a single cord. Any moment now it would crash to the ground. Other people saw that too. Looking up, they realised the danger, and ran, screaming, disappearing into the smoke.

But there were people who couldn't run. A young woman struggled to free herself – but her legs were pinned under some kind of steel panel. She could see the beam too. It swung almost above her head. I saw the fear in her eyes, the panic as she tried to pull herself free.

Emir Khan was dragging me on. 'Come on!'

But I couldn't leave her. No one else seemed to have noticed her. They were all running through the smoke, terrified of another explosion. I jerked free of the reporter's grip, jumped down the stairs towards her. She had begun to scream, couldn't stop screaming, couldn't take her eyes off that beam. I glanced up again. It was swaying to and fro, to and fro, the steel cord supporting it ready to snap at any second.

At last I reached her. I bent over her and whispered, 'I'll help you.'

Then, with all the strength I had, I tried to lift the panel from her legs. Smoke was engulfing the whole concourse. I swallowed clouds of it, could taste it, feel it winding its way down into my lungs. No matter how I tried I couldn't lift that panel. I was too young. I didn't have enough strength.

She was crying now, tears streaking her dusty face. I saw despair fill her eyes. There had to be someone here who could help me. Where was Emir? People came and went, vanishing through the smoke like ghosts. It was almost as if we were the only ones left in the world.

She gripped my sleeve. 'My baby,' she said, and for the first time I noticed her bump. Was that what gave me the strength I needed? I don't know. I only knew I had to save her then. I took one deep breath, and lifted. I thought my back was going to break, but at last I could feel the panel rise . . . by a few centimetres. I heard her gasp. *Get out now!* I wanted to shout it to her – had no breath to speak. But, desperate to save her baby, she knew. She rolled away – rolled so far she disappeared into the dust and the smoke and was gone.

I let the panel smash to the ground and turned to look for Emir Khan. There was no sign of him, no sign of anyone. And then a hand appeared through the brown mist, like something ghostly. A voice cried weakly, 'Help.'

I ran towards the hand, clutched it tight. It was an old blue-veined hand, wrinkled and bony. Now I could make out a face: an old man's face, twisted in pain. I tried to help him stand. He let out a painful moan and shook his head.

For a second the smoke cleared and I could see his legs. One of them was bent at a strange angle just below the knee. Broken.

Rage rushed from me. I was angry at whoever could have done this thing to him, to an old man, to a woman expecting a baby, to all these innocent people.

No one had the right!

I looked around. My eyes nipped. I could feel smoky fingers reaching down into my stomach. I was coughing. I would have to pull the old man away from here, drag him to safety.

'This might hurt,' I said softly. I put my hands under his arms and began to slide him back. The beam above us still swung precariously. I had so little time.

The old man winced with pain but managed to whisper, 'I'm fine, I'm fine', trying to be brave, not wanting me to stop. And I couldn't stop.

His mouth fell open and for a moment I thought he had died. Then he let out such a sigh of pain I could hardly bear it. I dragged him back, as far from the beam as I could. I heard the wails of the police cars and ambulances already approaching.

Suddenly, the steel cord snapped. The beam tumbled. I looked up and watched it as it fell, almost in slow motion. It crashed to the ground, bounced and crashed again, where the pregnant girl had been, where the old man had lain.

I bent down to him. He lay still, but opened his eyes and even managed the hint of a smile. 'Thank you . . .' he said softly. 'I won't forget you . . .'

There was nothing else I could do. The paramedics would be here soon. Someone would help him, someone more capable than me.

I stepped away. There was no sign of Emir Khan. No sign of anyone. Just dust and smoke and noise and confusion.

A terrible fear overtook me.

The world had changed.

If I ran now into the street, there would be the same chaos. And not just in the street. The chaos would be everywhere. It would never stop.

I saw bridges blown up, planes exploding in the sky,

others crashing into buildings. I saw it as if I was watching a movie in my head.

There would be no escape from this nightmare. Everywhere I would turn it would be the same. In every city, in every country. Nowhere would be safe. People would be dying in their hundreds, in their thousands.

And there was nothing I could do. Nothing anyone could do.

What was happening to me? Was I dreaming? Was I remembering? Because that terror I could see happen in my head was so real, I couldn't move. My head was spinning, the world was spinning around me. But I couldn't move.

I had never been so afraid.

Yes . . . you have.

From somewhere deep within me a voice whispered it.

Yes, you have been so afraid.

Maybe then I would have remembered everything; maybe that was the moment when it was all going to come back to me. But in that same second, Emir seemed to appear out of nowhere.

'I thought I'd lost you. Come on! We have to get out of here.'

The world came back into focus. There was uproar and confusion all around us – people running, calling for help, screaming in panic.

I ran after Emir. I wanted to haul him back, tell him: *We can't leave here. It's the same everywhere. No escape.*

But I couldn't speak.

I was running, but I was in another time, another place.

Through the smoke a memory became clearer. Some time ago I had been in a place like this. A dark place. Confused and frightened, and running. Running from another explosion.

I was running from the London bomb – it was the only other explosion I knew about.

But how would I have been caught up in that? What did I know about it? I had been there, in that explosion. Why?

I stopped dead, frozen, even in the midst of all this. I was desperate to snatch something from my past. I had been there, running in terror away from him, and I couldn't think why or how. What terrible thing was my memory trying to push towards me? Remember. *Remember*.

Emir grabbed my arm. He must have seen how my eyes were glazed. 'Come on, boy. You don't understand. We have to get out of here.' His voice became soft, as if someone might be listening. 'That bomb was meant for you and me.'

09

Everyone was panicking. There was a tidal wave of bodies trying desperately to get out of the station. I kept my eyes glued to Emir Khan. I knew if I took my eyes off him for a moment, I would lose sight of him completely.

Too many people trying to get out. I felt my legs being lifted off the ground by the power of the crowd. I was losing my balance. I was terrified. I had no control over my body as it was lifted and carried. I was going under, dragged by an undertow, just as if I was drowning.

'Emir Khan!' I yelled out his name, hoping he would hear me over the panicked noises. I knew I only had a few seconds before I was trampled, crushed by the crowd. How could I hope he would hear me over all this?

And then strong hands gripped my shoulders, plucked me free. This time he held my arm tight, wouldn't let go. The smoke was clearing. I could see the sky. We were outside. There was pandemonium in the street too: ambulances arriving, people stumbling out of the station, frightened and disorientated. Emir kept pulling me along.

'My car's parked round the corner,' he said breathlessly.

No one tried to stop us. We raced away from the station and down a side street. It was quieter there, away from the crowds. Emir ran up to a red car and fumbled with his keys. His hands were shaking as he opened the door. The blast had scared him too.

I threw myself into the front passenger seat. A moment later we were roaring away from the devastation and the carnage, heading out of the city.

'Where are we going?' I asked him.

'As far away from here as we can,' he said. 'Somewhere safe.'

But where was safe?

'What did you mean, that was meant for me and you?'

He took his eyes off the road to look at me. 'Everyone who thinks there's a conspiracy dies. They've been after me for a long time. Must have known I was meeting you. You and me. It looks like we're the only ones left.'

'Who knew I was meeting you?' I asked him. 'Did you tell anyone?'

He concentrated on the road again, winding his way through the narrow back streets heading out of the city. 'I think my phone's bugged. It's been done before.'

I didn't want to ask the next question, but I had to. 'The someone else you were meeting at the station . . . do you think they got her?'

This time he didn't look at me, just kept staring ahead. 'Yes. I'm afraid so. Three birds with one bomb. You and her, and me too. I've always been a thorn in their flesh.'

'Who's they?' I asked.

'The people behind all this.'

'Behind all what? What's their plan? Do you know?'

'I was hoping you might be able to tell me that.'

I almost smiled. Almost, but not quite. For I could still see in my mind that trapped woman, and the old man reaching out to me. Still hear the screams. No time for smiling. And anyway, how could I tell him anything?

'I know nothing,' I told him. 'I've lost my memory.'

He didn't seem surprised or disappointed. A witness who could remember nothing. Maybe he was used to people with amnesia.

'But I think I was caught up with that other explosion. It keeps coming back to me. The Lone Bomber. I think I was there.'

Now he looked at me. 'You remember being there?'

'Now and again I remember something. Like when we were running back then, through the smoke, something came to me. I think I was remembering running from that other explosion. Maybe I saw something that day.'

He didn't say anything for a time, and then, 'We'll stop soon. We'll talk about it then. I just want to get as far away from here as possible. I hope no one's following us.'

The bomb was meant for me. Me and that other witness. I kept seeing the black woman as she caught sight of me. Was she the other witness?

She was dead now, probably, and I would never know. How many other people were dead?

35

And how many people did they, all the Dark Men, intend to kill?

For now I was sure there was a whole army of Dark Men out there.

10

11 A.M.

'Where are we going?' We were on the motorway. I saw the signs leading us west, towards Glasgow.

'I think I know someone who could help you; I'm taking you to him.' Emir Khan kept glancing in the mirror. 'I don't think we're being followed.'

I turned my head to look. There was a huge truck coming up behind us, too close. I had a glimpse of a blue car somewhere behind that. Apart from that, the motorway seemed Sunday quiet.

'Do you really think we could be being followed?'

'Someone will have been watching. I think they'll try.'

'I've been followed all the way,' I told him. 'He's found me everywhere I go.'

'Who has?'

How could I tell him I called him the Dark Man? Sounded idiotic when I spoke the name aloud, and to an adult. 'I don't know his name.' I remembered then I had something better than a name. I patted my pockets. 'But I have a photo.'

That did shake him. His head turned sharply. 'You have a photo?'

'That's the reason I definitely know there is a conspiracy. He's with the Lone Bomber.'

He could only glance for a second at the picture. I could tell he wanted to look at it more closely. 'There's a lay-by up ahead. I think we'll head for that. I have to see this.'

He drew to a halt and I watched the truck and then the blue car zoom past. Through the tinted glass I couldn't even see the driver. No one seemed interested in us.

I handed the photo to Emir, watched his face as he studied it. I pointed to the Dark Man. 'Do you know him?'

He shook his head. 'But this one.' He indicated the man in the middle. 'This is definitely the Lone Bomber. Who's the other man?'

'His name was Gallacher.' It hurt even thinking about Ryan's dad. The sight of his eyes as he was dragged to his doom would never leave me, still too fresh in my memory not to hurt. How I wished I could forget it. 'He was part of a sleeper cell. That's why I know it must be a conspiracy. There are sleeper cells all over the country. They were all in it together. I just don't know why.'

'And they were both in the army with the bomber . . . That's right, he served in the Gulf. They said he suffered from Gulf War Syndrome; he was invalided out of the army and given a desk job, but his condition worsened. He became increasingly paranoid and ended up on indefinite leave. He lost his family, his job. It came as no surprise to anyone he planted the bomb.'

'But he wasn't working on his own.'

Emir stared at me. 'No. Not on his own. He was what they call *the patsy*.'

'The patsy?' I didn't understand what that meant.

'The fool who takes the blame,' Emir said simply. 'The man who shot JFK, Lee Harvey Oswald, he was a patsy too. Another conspiracy theory – never solved.'

'We'll solve this one, won't we?'

'Now we have you . . . and this photograph, I hope so.'

I would have preferred him to sound more certain. 'There's something coming,' I said. 'Something big. Gallacher was part of a sleeper cell; there are sleeper cells all over the country, waiting, just waiting. Maybe the Lone Bomber was part of a sleeper cell, but he was a loose cannon. He couldn't wait, planted his bomb too soon. And I saw something, know something about it, and that's why I'm dangerous.'

Who was I?

'I wish I could remember.' I hadn't realised I had spoken it aloud. Until Emir Khan answered me.

'I know a doctor. He uses hypnosis. He specialises in releasing locked-in memories.' He pulled out again on to the road.

'You really think this doctor can help me remember?'

'I know he can.'

I was going to remember. I wanted to remember everything. I wanted to find out who the Dark Man really was, and how I was linked to all this. I wanted to know who I was.

I was shaking. The explosion had affected me more

than I realised. Emir glanced at me. 'You've been through a lot. Are you hungry?'

Was I hungry? I was always hungry. I nodded.

'There's a motel up ahead,' Emir said. 'We'll check in there. You look as if you need to clean up too. I'll get you something to eat and phone the doctor, see if he can meet up with us. We need to find out what it is you know.'

The boy didn't even notice the blue car pulling out after them at the next junction. His mind seemed to be on other things. The Dark Man smiled, kept a steady pace behind them, leaving just enough cars in front.

He was closing in again.

11

ROBIN HOOD MOTEL, the neon sign proclaimed, still lit up on this dark winter morning. Only thing was some of the letters weren't working, so it actually read: *BIN HO D MO L.*

Sounded more like a Chinese gangster to me. I waited in the car as Emir Khan booked us in.

I wasn't alone any more. That's all I kept thinking. I wasn't alone any more.

He needed to call this doctor, he told me, and make arrangements for me to meet him, hopefully some time today. It seemed Emir was in as much of a hurry as I was.

It was such a dark gloomy day, matching my mood. My thoughts kept going back to the railway station. How many had been killed? The woman at the news-stand? Was she alive? As I sat waiting for Emir, a line of multicoloured bulbs flashed above the covered walkway around the cabins. Would we be safe here? I didn't feel safe, but when did I ever?

Emir came hurrying out of the office, keys dangling from his fingers. 'Cabin thirteen,' he said, sliding into the driver's seat. 'Lucky for some.'

Cabin thirteen was clean but basic: two single beds, a

fitted wardrobe with a high shelf stuffed with extra blankets, a bathroom with a shower, tea-making facilities, a television and not much else. I made for the tea straight away while Emir switched on the radiator.

'I'm sorry,' Emir said. 'I should have realised you'd be hungry. I'll go and see if I can get you something more substantial than biscuits.' He took his phone from his pocket. 'I want to try and call this doctor anyway. He lives not far from here. Doctor Lloyd, that's his name. He's discreet, and he owes me a favour.'

I wasn't sure I knew what discreet meant, but I knew all about being owed a favour.

As soon as he left I switched on the TV and checked out the bathroom. The shower looked tempting. And there was a pile of thick clean towels on a stainless steel shelf above the bath. I had time, I thought, while Emir was off getting me some food. The thought of hot water was making me giddy. I stripped off quickly and let the hot spray wash over my face and my body. I could have stayed there for ever.

Emir still wasn't back by the time I came out of the bathroom. I had warmed my clothes over the radiator, and once I was dressed again, I felt snugger than I had for an age. I lay on the bed, my hands curled round a mug of hot tea, to watch the news. I wanted to find out everything about the bombing.

The set was an old one and the picture was fuzzy. The main story was the explosion at the station. A reporter stood in front of a scene of chaos. Behind him, police and paramedics carried the injured out on stretchers, or helped stumbling people into ambulances.

Miraculously, no one had been killed. I had never felt so relieved. It seemed a woman had noticed a suspicious briefcase just in time, and that warning had saved many lives.

No one had been killed.

That meant that the woman who had come to meet Emir Khan was still alive too.

No one had been killed.

But what kind of horrific injuries had they survived with?

I was so angry I could have yelled out. What right had anyone to plant a bomb, to maim and kill innocent people going about their ordinary lives?

'*The government has raised the security risk level to critical because of today's bombing. A police spokesman announced just a few minutes ago that detectives were not ruling out a possible connection between the bombing here at Waverley Station and the kidnapping of MP Angus Lennox's daughter.*'

The area behind the reporter was cordoned off with yellow tape. The camera closed in on him for effect. '*This morning's dramatic events will no doubt add to rising pressure on the government to take action against an escalating number of terrorist attacks, as the public calls for more drastic measures to be taken. And while world leaders decide how to respond to these demands at a major conference being held at Hanover House, thousands of peace protesters prepare to take part in a series of marches across the country tomorrow, in a united stand against terrorism.*'

The camera panned back. The reporter's tone changed.

'*But even within the chaos, in the aftermath of today's explosion, there have been reports of bravery. Several survivors have spoken about a boy who seemed to come out of the smoke and save them. He dragged one eighty-two-year-old man to safety, and lifted a heavy steel beam from a young pregnant woman. And then –*' the reporter blew across the open palm of his hand – '*he was gone. Who was he? Do you know this boy? A number of people are keen to meet him and thank him.*'

I lay on my stomach on the bed, fascinated. *I* was that mysterious boy!

'*Or was he even real?*' the reporter went on. '*A porter who has worked at this station for several years has another theory.*' He held the mike out to an older, uniformed man. '*Mr Maxwell, tell us who you think this boy was.*'

Mr Maxwell looked a bit nervous in front of the camera. He fiddled with his tie before he spoke. '*He's the station ghost,*' the porter stated with authority.

This was getting better by the minute. First I was a mysterious hero, now I was a ghost.

'*Years ago,*' this Mr Maxwell went on, his confidence growing as he spoke, '*many years ago, there was a crash in the station. A boy and his mother were on the train – the mother was killed. But they think the pair must have got separated at some point, because this young boy went around the train helping people, but all the time he was asking if anyone had seen his mother. It was only later they discovered both their bodies, in different parts of the train. The boy had died during the crash too. But since then, there's been several reports that he's been seen wandering about the station, still looking for his mother.*'

The reporter turned from Mr Maxwell back to the camera. '*So a ghost, or a real-life hero?*'

A huge weight of sadness fell on me then . . . because I didn't know what I was either. A ghost, searching for my mother? I was certainly searching for something, aching to find someone who cared about me, aching to feel safe at last.

The reporter wasn't finished yet. '*A mystery boy has been popping up in several news stories over the past couple of weeks. In a west coast town a boy was reported to have brought to justice a notorious hitman known as the Wolf before disappearing again. And just a couple of days ago, there was the front-page news of the rescue of many people from a secret underground bunker. They had been drugged and kidnapped and kept there by a man calling himself the Reaper. All of them swear it was a boy who led them through the bunker to safety, but no trace of their rescuer has been found.*'

That was me too, the boy always disappearing into the shadows. Maybe one day I would be able to walk into the light.

I remembered Faisal and Kirsten saying I had become an urban legend. Was that what I was? An urban legend? A myth?

The reporter handed back to the studio presenters. The newsreader's voice was suitably grim.

'*Now for other news, and there's been another twist in the kidnapping of Sapphire Lennox.*'

Pictures of a rather dour-looking man flashed on the screen. He had tufty red hair fading to grey and wore thick glasses – a renowned politician, the reporter was saying.

'*Sapphire Lennox has been missing for five days. Her father, MP Angus Lennox, has now had a demand from the group who claim to be holding her for the release of all terrorist suspects in British prisons. Angus Lennox has been a vociferous critic of the present government's policies on terrorism, and colleagues of the politician say he has made a lot of enemies both here and abroad. The kidnappers, whose identities are still not known, are threatening to execute Sapphire if their demands are not met by twelve noon tomorrow.*'

The daughter appeared on the screen. Her hair was blonde and curly, and her eyes were as sapphire blue as her name. She was flashing a glossy-lipped smile at the cameras as she hurried into some London nightclub. She looked familiar. Probably from magazine covers from my forgotten past.

Now the footage showed Angus Lennox as he pushed his way through a throng of reporters and photographers. I'd seen his face somewhere before too.

The politician had a mike pushed into his face.

'*Have you anything to say to your daughter's kidnappers, Mr Lennox?*'

At this he spoke directly into the camera, as if he was talking to me. '*I can only say one thing. Let my daughter go. She is a complete innocent. She doesn't deserve this. Please . . . I'm no threat to you. You have my word.*' Then he pushed the microphone away as if he'd said too much. He looked ready to cry.

He was pleading to the kidnappers, in case they might be watching the same newscast. Did kidnappers do that? I wondered – ordinary things like watching television?

I looked away from the screen.

What was keeping Emir? He was supposed to be buying me a burger, not having to round up the cow and make it himself.

He was taking a long time over one call.

12

12.30 P.M.

Greta pushed open the door of the apartment. She called out, but she knew already that her boss wasn't there. She had been knocking for a good few minutes, and no answer. She didn't usually work on a Sunday, but she was having her day off tomorrow instead. She wanted to go on the peace march too. Good thing he had given her the keys. She went about her business, cleaning up in the kitchen first. He had left a half-eaten pizza on the table beside the phone. The man did not eat properly, she was thinking. What he needed was a wife. Greta dreamt sometimes that she was his wife – had dreamt about finding a husband like him since she was a little girl in Poland. She threw the remains of the pizza in the bin. It looked as if he had left in a hurry. He always seemed to be receiving calls and rushing off somewhere in search of a story. It could be exciting working for him. She hoped he would take her back to London with him when he left, find he just couldn't do without her.

Sometimes, however, it was not so exciting, like when he would leave his dirty washing lying about, just like her brothers back home.

Men – the same the world over.

There were crumbs all over the floor too, and pieces of pizza, and then she noticed a broken glass. Either he had had too much to drink – and she had not known that to be the case since she had been working for him – or his phone call had been so exciting that he had swept the glass off the table by accident.

Whatever the reason, Greta was the one who would have to clean it up.

With a long sigh, Greta crossed into the hall to get the vacuum cleaner out of the cupboard. She opened the door – and screamed.

I held open the blinds and peered outside. Emir was still on the phone, wandering up and down the open walkway, intent on his conversation. I was just about to lower the blinds and step away from the window, when I saw a blue car with tinted windows cruise silently into the motel car park . . . so silent, as if the engine had been switched off and it was freewheeling. I had seen that car before, behind us on the motorway.

I was about to tap on the window to alert Emir, when I saw his almost imperceptible gesture as he raised a finger to acknowledge the car driver's presence.

Greta pulled herself together almost at once. No time for panic, or for screaming. She took a deep breath and lifted the red baseball cap from his face. She wanted to cry. But she held back her tears. It was her boss all right, Emir Khan. And he was dead.

The man calling himself Emir Khan stepped into cabin thirteen again. 'I'm back,' he called. 'Got some fish and chips – hope that's OK.'

The television was on, too loud. The bathroom door was closed. He could hear the shower running. He looked back and beckoned the Dark Man inside the room, motioning to him with a nod of his head to the bathroom.

'No window,' he mouthed.

They moved forward swiftly. The Dark Man put his shoulder to the door. It crashed open and they both almost fell inside.

The bathroom was empty. The Dark Man snapped the shower curtain across so roughly some of the rings whipped off and rattled across the tiled floor. He pushed the other man aside, ran out of the bathroom. The bedroom window was slightly open, curtains fluttering in the breeze. The only other way out. He slipped it wide and his lean frame was outside in a second. The other man tumbled out after him, saying, 'He can't have gone far. There's nowhere for him to go.'

A truck was pulling out on to the motorway. The Dark Man watched it and almost ran to his car, ready to follow after it.

Something stopped him. Surely the boy hadn't had time to make it to that truck. He was still around some-where. He was convinced of it.

13

'He can't have gone far.'

The two men had returned to the motel room. It was the man I had called Khan who was speaking.

'I only left him for a moment.' *Bit of a lie there*, I thought. 'I can't understand how he sussed us out. He was totally fooled, really believed I was this Emir Khan.'

His words gushed out of him. He was afraid of the Dark Man. I could hear it in his voice.

'He's not a boy easily fooled, Salou,' the Dark Man snapped. So his name was Salou. 'Something made him suspicious.'

The Dark Man's voice made me shiver; it brought back memories of him whispering to me. Whispering what, and why? I could never hold on to those memories.

'He has to be here somewhere,' Salou insisted. 'I mean, he's only a boy.' There was a challenge in the way he said it. 'I almost had him.'

'Almost isn't good enough.'

Salou didn't say a word for a moment. The animosity between the two men filled the silence.

'We're going to search here. Look everywhere,' the Dark Man said. 'If he's here, we'll find him.'

Jane Faulkner opened her eyes. The nurse beside her smiled, urged her to sleep again. 'You need rest,' she said softly.

Jane couldn't think where she was at first. The room was dark, with a strange green light in the corner – a machine of some kind. Hospital . . .

She tried to remember. She'd been waiting for someone, waiting in a railway station. She'd been waiting for that reporter, Emir Khan.

There was a case lying by her feet. She could picture it now: a hard black briefcase with gold locks, left there by some absent-minded businessman, she had thought at first. She remembered becoming suspicious . . . stepping away to report it, walking round the corner to look for someone from security or the rail network. She had found one, and he had listened to her, immediately ordered people to get back . . . and then . . .

She began to move, to struggle to her feet, and the pain shot through her shoulder. She was bandaged, a drip in her arm; she couldn't get out of the bed.

The nurse moved closer. 'It's OK, Miss Faulkner.' She put a calming hand on hers. 'You're not badly hurt. You're going to be fine. You're one of the lucky ones.'

But Jane would not be calmed. She tried to talk, but her mouth was thick and the words wouldn't come. She wanted to say she wasn't one of the lucky ones. That bomb had been meant for her. And she was still alive and they knew it.

They would come back for her.

They had spent too much time searching for him, and he was nowhere. The Dark Man was angry. He thought of the truck again. He must have made that truck after all. And he hadn't even got the registration.

There was a lot to do. He couldn't waste any more time here. He headed back to the motel room.

'I'll get him next time,' Salou said, as if to himself as he stepped into the room after the Dark Man.

The Dark Man turned on him. 'There won't be a next time for you. The boy's mine. It would do well for you not to forget that.'

He wanted rid of Salou. He hadn't wanted him involved in the first place.

'Did you speak to the doctor?'

Salou answered. 'Yes, I told him we'd bring the boy to him. But what's the use in going now if we don't have the boy?'

The Dark Man ignored that question. 'I have to go. There are other things I have to do. I'll find the boy again. I always find him.'

'After tomorrow it won't matter, will it? Doesn't matter what he knows.'

'It still matters. You don't know how much it matters. And our best bet is to let the doctor work his magic on him.'

He would not kill the boy. Not yet. He was

disobeying orders here, but he had his reasons.

'I'll wait here. He has to be here somewhere,' Salou said.

'You also have other things to do. The woman, Jane Faulkner, is still alive.' His tone said that had been a bad mistake. 'Find out which hospital she's in. I think you should go and finish off what you were supposed to do. And this time . . . do it right.'

'That wasn't my fault,' Salou began, but the Dark Man ignored him. 'And anyway, she won't matter tomorrow either.'

'She's a loose end,' the Dark Man said. 'And I do not like loose ends.'

'And what about our little treasure?' Salou asked sarcastically.

'We've put that somewhere appropriate, let's say. Somewhere no one will ever find it.'

Salou laughed. 'That should teach someone to keep their mouth shut.'

The Dark Man ignored him. He was already leaving the room. 'Pay up here and move fast.'

He paused for a moment outside. 'The truck,' he muttered. The boy had been quicker than he thought. He must have made that truck.

14

1.30 P.M.

But the boy hadn't made the truck. The boy hadn't even left the room.

And the boy had heard their every word.

I had not dared move a muscle as I had lain there, tucked into the shelf in the fitted wardrobe, a couple of blankets in front of me. When I saw that Emir Khan knew the Dark Man I had to think fast. He had come for me. I was sure I didn't have time to get out of the room and run, get away from him. The running shower, the open window – misdirection I prayed would fool them, and it had. And because I had risked hiding here, I had heard everything. 'It won't matter tomorrow,' Salou had said. *It* was happening tomorrow. But where? What?

I was angry with myself. I should have guessed soon-er that Emir Khan was a fake. In the confusion at the station I had forgotten all about the red baseball cap he was supposed to have been wearing. And I had already told him about the photograph when I'd called, so why had he been so surprised? *Close call, Ram*, I thought.

But he hadn't lied about a doctor. There was a doctor

who could 'work his magic' on me. I wondered exactly what that magic was. Maybe they needed to know what was locked in my head as much as I did.

I waited till I was sure they had left and then almost fell out of the shelf. My bones ached with lying in such a cramped position for so long. I lay on the floor for a moment, trying to get the feeling back in my legs, trying to make sense of what I had heard them say.

The Dark Man had been going somewhere, he had things to do – things that concerned what was going to happen tomorrow.

And there was another clue. Someone was being taught a lesson in how to keep their mouth shut. And something had been put somewhere no one would ever find it. I couldn't understand any of that.

What I did understand was that Emir Khan was dead. And the man, Salou, who had pretended to be him had been sent off to 'finish the job'. What job was that? Jane Faulkner was still alive, the Dark Man had said, and she was a loose end he wanted cleared up. She was supposed to have died in that explosion. That bomb hadn't been meant for me. It had been meant for her. But for some reason, she was still alive . . . that was the job Salou had been sent to finish.

He was going to kill Jane Faulkner. How was I going to stop that?

Detective Inspector John Julian – JJ to his friends, though he didn't have too many of those – studied Emir Khan's room, working out exactly what had happened.

56

Someone had come to his door. He had let them in. Had he known his killer? He had put his phone number in the paper, a stupid thing to do in JJ's opinion, and he had asked people to contact him. Perhaps someone had come to his door pretending they too had a story. Instead they had a gun. It would have been quick. A bullet in the head – an assassin's shot – and then Emir's body had been stuffed in a cupboard so it would not be found, not right away. The killer probably didn't know the maid would be coming today.

Still, most professional killers did a better job at getting rid of the body than sticking it in a cupboard. Perhaps whoever had done this had been in a hurry to go somewhere else. But where?

And why had Khan been killed?

Not because of those articles, surely? JJ had read them, and dismissed Khan's speculation as incredible. It was too far-fetched a conspiracy theory, even for the detective. Yet, Emir Khan was dead. Had he hit some nerve with his articles?

The flat was being checked. His people had not been happy about how thorough he wanted them to be. He knew how professional they were, though he seldom told them that. He had a reputation for being gruff and unfriendly, the man who never smiled. But this was how he got results.

He lifted a small notebook that was lying on the desk by the phone, and flicked through it. The last entries:

Jane Faulkner.

The boy with no name. 10 a.m.

Jane Faulkner. That name rang a bell. Hadn't someone mentioned her only that morning . . . in connection with the bomb at Waverley Station?

But who was the boy with no name?

'OK,' he said, and he didn't miss the look of despair on his officers' faces. They all knew what he was about to say. 'Go over the flat one more time.'

15

It all seemed hopeless. I knew something was going to happen tomorrow, I just didn't know what or where. I could stop it if I could only remember.

I had so much information in my head, and yet I knew so little. And there was so much to do. Where to start?

I knew who murdered Emir Khan, knew where the phoney Emir Khan, this Salou, was headed and what he intended to do.

Kill Jane Faulkner.

Could I save her at least?

Maybe I could tell the man who ran the motel to phone the police.

No. He would be more likely to get them to come for me. And I couldn't have that. They would never believe my story anyway. And could I trust them? But who would listen to me, believe me? Me, the boy with no name? No memory? How long would it all take?

By the time anyone took me seriously, Jane Faulkner would be pushing up the daisies. If only there was some other way to warn them. I didn't even know what hospital she was in.

I knew nothing. Despair folded round me like

a blanket.

Maybe I should have let Salou and the Dark Man catch me – let this doctor 'work his magic' on me. I had no friends anyway. I knew nobody. Didn't even know my own name. Was it only this morning I thought I had found a friend, someone I could trust, someone who believed me?

Emir Khan.

I did know one thing. I knew his phone number.

Had they found his body yet? Would anyone be there in his flat? If they had, they would have to listen to what I had to tell them.

My eyes locked on the phone by the beds. Surely it was worth a try.

I was going to call Emir Khan's number.

16

2 P.M.

The forensic people were going through the flat one more time when the phone rang. They all stopped, looked at JJ. After a few rings he crossed to the desk, covered his hand with a cloth – though the phone had already been dusted for any fingerprints – and lifted the receiver.

He said nothing, waited.

'Who's that?' It was a boy's voice, breathless, almost a whisper. 'Who am I speaking to?'

'My name is Detective Inspector John Julian,' JJ said.

'You've already found his body, then?'

The boy knew he had been killed. 'Who are you?'

There was a hesitation. 'Doesn't matter. But I know who killed him, I know why – and I know who's next.'

'Who is this?'

I heard a door slam along the corridor. Someone was coming, would be here soon. I had no time to waste. So

61

why did this policeman with his gruff voice keep asking questions I had no time to answer?

'Doesn't matter who I am.' How could I tell him when I didn't know myself. 'Someone's coming to kill Jane Faulkner. She's in real danger. He's coming to the hospital. An Asian guy. I heard them calling him Salou.'

'I know who Jane Faulkner is,' John Julian said. 'I can find her.'

'You have to save her.'

'We will. Now who are you?'

I was glad the man didn't ask how I knew about Jane, as if he believed me instinctively. I wished I could tell him everything then. If only there was time. But the footsteps were coming closer. I had no time for explanations. I had to find the Dark Man.

I glanced at the door. Someone was right outside. I could hear the jangle of keys. Any second now the handle would turn, the door would open. No time to stay.

John Julian thought for a moment he'd been cut off. 'Hello? Hello? Tell me who you are,' he asked again.

'Hello? Who am I? I'm the service maid. Who are you? Has somebody been using this phone?'

It was a girl's voice.

'Is there a boy there?'

'Nobody's here. A man checked into this room on his own. And that man checked out, just about fifteen minutes ago. The phone was off the hook when I came in.'

The girl told him where she was speaking from, a

motel off the M8. But there was no sign of the boy.

Where was he? And why was he running? Why couldn't he wait there till someone came for him? . . . *The boy with no name.* JJ lifted Khan's notepad again. Had he just been speaking to the boy with no name?

Salou – now he knew he'd heard that name before. On a list of terror suspects.

He turned to one of the police officers. 'Find out which hospital Jane Faulkner is in and call me as soon as you know. I'm heading there now.'

Jane Faulkner. She was one of the women injured in today's bombing. The woman who had alerted security – who had probably saved a lot of lives.

Now they were after her. She knew something important, something they didn't want anyone else to know.

Today's bombing, a murder, now a woman in danger and a boy with no name.

JJ had no time to waste.

I had slipped out of the window just in time, heard the girl talking to this John Julian. I had to get away from there. Which direction had the Dark Man taken? I headed for the front of the motel, scouring the ground for tyre marks. Salou's car had been parked right outside the cabin. I saw the tyre marks from his car lead away from the motel and turn back east – in the direction of Edinburgh, and the hospitals.

The blue car, the Dark Man's car – I could see those tyre marks head steadily towards the exit west, towards Glasgow.

Why was he going that way?

That's the way I would go too.

I jumped into some bushes beside the slip road as I heard a truck behind me coming out of the petrol station. Rock music was thumping from the cabin, where I could make out two people: the driver, just a boy himself, and beside him a girl about my own age. They didn't see me. I let the truck pass, then I began to run. It would slow as it slipped on to the motorway. That would be my chance. I put on a spurt and leapt for the back, hung on for my life. The truck hardly slowed at all as it joined the motorway; it swerved so fast I was almost flung off. I took a deep breath, hauled myself over and dropped down.

17

I slumped to the floor of the truck, exhausted. It didn't matter where I was going, as long as it was in the same direction as the Dark Man.

Tomorrow.

What was going to happen tomorrow? Another explosion like the one today? Yet how would tomorrow's explosion be so important? Was it something to do with those marches that were planned?

I covered my face with my hands and tried to think.

No chance. Not the way this guy was driving.

I was almost thrown to the other side of the truck as it swerved again. I heard a horn blasting angrily from another car and my head banged on the metal bars behind me. If only a knock on the head would bring my memory back. But I'd had plenty of those and still nothing came. Everything I needed to know was in my mind somewhere, locked tight in there. I needed help. I needed someone who could probe my mind, unlock those memories.

The truck veered again. With this kind of driving I might not survive till tomorrow. I stood up and clung on to the bar on the wall to stop myself from falling.

Something moved, scraping on the floor in the shadows at the upper end of the truck.

I blinked, tried to make out what it was. The far end was cloaked in darkness. I could make out a tarpaulin. It seemed to be covering something that was tied up against the side of the wall. I could see there were ropes binding it. We swerved again. I kept my feet, wrapping my arm tighter round the bar. I peered closer. Something was definitely moving, sliding towards me.

And at last I made out what it was.

Couldn't believe what I was seeing.

It was a coffin.

18

It was dark in the room. Jane Faulkner opened her eyes. She could just see the clock on the wall and hear the light sounds of the hospital: footfalls in the corridor, someone coughing in another ward, a bell ringing for one of the nurses. She wished she was somewhere else, didn't want to be there. She was afraid. They all knew she was afraid – the nurses, the doctors; they thought it had to be the after-effects of the explosion. Post-traumatic stress, they would call it.

She wanted to tell them why she was so afraid. She knew she was next. They would be after her. But the words wouldn't come, and when she grew agitated trying to speak, they only gave her more drugs to calm her. The drugs made her sway in and out of consciousness. Yet she had to stay awake, watching for them, listening for them.

The coffin moved again. With every bump in the road, with every bend, it slid ever closer. I had backed up against the end of the truck; I couldn't take my eyes from it.

It made me remember the ghost I had seen in the graveyard. Maybe she had followed me, that strange figure with her long dark hair covering her face. I could picture her eyes, eyes I had never seen, staring at me through that thick mane of hair. Eyes without a soul. I saw her hands reaching out to me again.

I stared at the coffin. I imagined her inside there, pushing at the lid. It would creak open and she would sit up slowly, turn to look at me, begin to climb out of the coffin and crawl towards me . . .

It was so real in my mind I began to sweat, remembering my terror in the open grave in that old deserted cemetery.

The truck lurched again. The coffin slid closer. Any second now – I was waiting for it to happen – the lid would fly open and *she* would be there.

19

3 P.M.

Salou had reached the hospital, parking his car a few streets away. He walked quickly towards the main entrance. He expected to be stopped at reception, had his story ready. His cover was that he was a medical student: he was wearing his white coat – even had the appropriate badge. But no one looked at him twice. He kept his head down anyway, aware of the CCTV cameras that were everywhere.

He took the stairs. Their intelligence had told him exactly where Jane Faulkner was. He reached her floor in minutes, and stepped out of the stairwell into the corridor. Curtains were drawn across the windows of the wards so that the patients could have an hour or so of quiet time before visiting hours began. Perfect.

Jane Faulkner would be found, he'd been told, in her own private room. He could already see it, three doors down.

He headed towards it.

I can't say how long I stood there, frozen to the spot. My eyes never moved from that coffin. Not until I heard another sound from the dark recesses of the truck. There was a sudden bump in the road, and something began to roll towards me.

I couldn't make out what it was, not in the dark. A ball of some kind? It bumped against the coffin and came to a halt behind it, out of my sight. I licked the sweat from my upper lip.

What was in this truck?

Another memory came into focus – of a story I must have read, or a film I had seen somewhere, some time, in that past life. A truck. A truck that transported a vampire's coffin. Dracula's coffin. *Dracula*. The vampire.

There was another lurch as the truck zigzagged round a bend. Whatever that round object was, it began to roll again, running round the edge of the coffin. Any moment now I would be able to see it.

A football?

Had to be a football.

I watched in horror as it rolled closer and came to a stop, centimetres from my feet.

It wasn't a football.

It was a disembodied head.

20

Footsteps.

Jane heard them approaching in the distance, coming down the corridor.

Not a woman. These were the heavy footsteps of a man, heading this way.

A doctor?

She tried to sit up but she couldn't move, as if she was strapped down. She wasn't though. It was the drugs that held her down. Her eyes followed the sound of the footsteps. And then they stopped. Right outside her room. A dark shadow filled the glass panel in the door.

She tried to stay conscious, tried to scream. Couldn't.

They had come.

The head lay at my feet. Blood was congealed round the neck. The eyes were still open and stared up at me. No wonder I hadn't been able to stop myself from yelling. I could feel my knees almost give way. If I could have moved, I'd have leapt from the back, taken the risk of being splattered all over the motorway.

Hang on . . .

The eyes still stared up at me.

There was something weird about those eyes. They were too glassy. Not so much dead eyes, as eyes that had never known life. I took a deep breath, stretched out my hand . . .

The hair was wiry. It wasn't real. The eyes weren't real.

I gripped the hair and lifted the head. It was as light as a feather. I looked inside. Nothing. It was hollow. A fake. And if it was a fake . . .

I stepped towards the coffin, fumbled with the catch on the lid.

I leapt back, almost yelled again as a skeleton sprang to a sitting position.

And then I laughed.

Whatever was in here was no danger to me, nothing to be afraid of. I walked unsteadily across to the far wall. What was under that sheet? As I lifted it, the tarpaulin slipped to the floor.

The giant open mouth of a monster gaped in front of me. I read the words above the mouth, words that dripped blood.

THE TUNNEL OF TERROR
ENTER AT YOUR PERIL

72

21

Salou crept towards her bed. He had a syringe in his hand ready to use – a lethal injection, virtually untraceable. He took a few steps into the room. Anyone seeing him would think he was just one of the doctors, with his white coat and stethoscope around his neck.

The figure in the bed shifted slightly. Even if Jane Faulkner saw him now, it wouldn't matter. It was too late. Too late for her anyway.

The figure turned. He saw the face.

Salou gasped, puzzled. The figure on the bed wasn't Jane Faulkner. It wasn't even a woman.

In fact, it wasn't a patient at all. The man threw the covers aside and leapt from the bed. It was a policeman.

'Grab him.' He didn't shout it, but immediately more police officers seemed to emerge from nowhere. Salou was pinioned by the arms.

'Watch that syringe!'

He tried desperately to turn it on one of the officers, or as a last resort on himself, but was forced to drop it from his fingers. He heard it shatter as it hit the tiled floor.

It was a trap. He had walked into a trap. How had they known?

He had failed again. Another failure would be unacceptable. He couldn't risk them questioning him. Salou relaxed in their grip, as if he had given up. He felt the two men holding him let go ever so slightly, just enough. He wrenched himself suddenly from their grip, kicked out with his feet, pushed them and began to run.

They were straight after him, their pounding feet breaking the silence of the hospital corridor. He glanced from left to right, saw then that the floor was empty. Empty beds, empty wards; patients moved while they waited for him to come. A whole floor evacuated. How had they known? he thought again. Was there a traitor among them?

He turned a corner, found himself in a long corridor. He didn't hesitate, tried the first door, then the second. Locked. The doors were all locked – no handy room to hide in, no emergency exit for him to leap through. Only a window at the end of the corridor.

He wouldn't be caught. He couldn't be caught. The only way out was the window. He was four floors up. Could he make it?

Did it matter?

He sprinted towards it. The police were just behind him, shouting now, beginning to understand what he was going to attempt but unable to stop him.

And he leapt, crashing through the glass. He crossed his arms in front of his face to protect it, but he could still feel the shards of glass biting into his skin. He didn't dare look down, four floors down, but there – suspended in the air for one moment – he knew he wasn't going to make it.

And it didn't matter. He had failed. If he'd gone back to them . . . they'd have killed him anyway.

22

'I hope the officer didn't frighten you earlier,' JJ said as he stepped into Jane's room.

Jane's eyes were fixed behind him on the officer's dark shadow filling the glass panel of the door, a look of terror, of utter helplessness on her face.

'I wanted to put a guard there,' JJ went on. 'Just in case.'

She struggled to speak. 'He came, didn't he?'

No point lying to her. 'Yes, he came. But we've caught him.' He didn't tell her the man was dead – killed himself rather than be arrested, questioned. What were they up against here? 'You're out of danger now.'

He stepped forward. Her eyes were filled with tears. He couldn't help noticing how dark her eyes were, how very beautiful.

He'd phoned the hospital on his mobile as soon as he'd found out where Jane Faulkner had been taken. He'd gone to see her, had her and all the other patients on her floor evacuated. Convincing his superiors on the word of some mystery boy's phone call hadn't been easy, but they'd agreed eventually. Couldn't afford not to. Thank God. The boy had been right about someone coming to kill Jane Faulkner, and the identity of that assassin. Salou. Known associate of any extremist organisation who would pay him.

JJ couldn't get the boy out of his mind – the boy with no name. The boy had been in danger, had sounded afraid. Would he be able to find him again? Would he be able to save him too? He could only hope the boy would call back.

JJ had heard all the conspiracy theories, but there was never any evidence to back them up. Like most people, he had thought them all tabloid inventions to sell papers.

But Jane Faulkner was lying in this hospital bed because she knew something. The boy with no name was afraid because he knew something.

Now JJ knew there was a conspiracy.

And it wasn't over yet.

'That was definitely a scream I heard, Shanti.' Barry, the driver, turned to the girl beside him.

How Barry could hear anything she didn't know, he had that music of his turned up so loud. If she'd known he liked his music as ear-drum-shattering as this, she'd have brought ear plugs along.

He turned down the music at last.

Shanti thought quickly. She didn't want Barry stopping to investigate. 'It wasn't a scream.' She pretended to glance into the side mirror. 'It was a boy racer. It was his tyres screeching.'

Luckily, she thought, Barry wasn't dealing with a full

pack. However, he still glanced in his side mirror.

'I can't see any boy racer.'

'He turned off at the last exit. Can't believe you didn't see him!'

'Did you tie that coffin down properly?'

Typical! It was always her that got the blame. 'Course I did! If something's come loose back there it's because of your rubbish driving.'

'I'm a good driver.' He took his eyes off the road to tell her that. The truck swerved once again.

'And I'm the Queen of Sheba.'

'See you, Shanti, you get on my wick. You're nothing but a moan.'

'OK, stop the truck and I'll go back and see.'

'No way! I'm not stopping till we get back. I've got a date tonight.'

'You mean you found somebody daft enough to go out with you?'

Barry swerved again as he glared at her. 'It's Michelle, I'll have you know.'

'Michelle? That explains it. She's got even fewer brain cells than you.'

'I'm quite a catch, I'll have you know.'

'So was Jaws,' Shanti snapped back. She couldn't let it go, loved winding him up. 'She's probably only going out with you to get free rides.'

Barry tried to think of a snappy retort to throw back at her, but he couldn't come up with anything.

'Well, it sounded like a scream to me,' he said again.

It had sounded like a scream to Shanti too. Someone was in the back of the truck – but she wasn't going to admit that to Barry. It seemed she had made another mistake. She hadn't tied the back up properly. Someone was there, probably some old tramp – they were always trying to hitch lifts.

Shanti made a mental note: as soon as they reached their destination she was going to chuck out whoever was in there before Uncle Ben found him. She couldn't afford for her uncle to find out she had screwed up again. She couldn't afford to make any more mistakes.

They might send her back.

Not that she could remember exactly where 'back' was . . . but it was definitely somewhere she didn't want to be.

23

4 P.M.

Barry swung the truck into the drive of the fairground. Shanti loved the fair, even in the daytime when it lay quiet, stalls covered, rides still. She always felt at home here. This was her life, and she loved it.

It wasn't quiet now though; stalls and booths were setting up as people passed through to visit the water festival and the tall ships berthed at the dock on the river.

It was going to be a busy night with so many people there preparing for the peace marches tomorrow.

She had been tense since she'd heard those noises in the back of the truck. As soon as Barry screeched to a halt – why did he always have to screech? – she had the passenger door open and was running to the back.

'I'll check in here, Barry. You let Uncle Ben know we're back.' She didn't have to tell Barry twice. He was always eager to avoid work that required any kind of heavy lifting. And anyway, he had a date, as he kept reminding her.

'OK, no problem, Shanti.'

Shanti waited till he was well out of sight before she

leapt into the back of the truck. She almost tripped over the coffin. So, it *had* moved. She looked around, could hardly see anything in the dark. The cover had slipped from the facade of the ghost train. Was that all that had happened here? Barry's erratic driving had loosened her ropes, sent everything slipping and sliding?

Then who had yelled?

No, there was something else. Someone else. She stood still . . . And could hear the sound of their soft breathing. They were still here.

'OK! Out! Now!'

It would only be some old tramp – they were always cadging lifts – a dosser, a down and out. Shanti wasn't afraid. She stood with her hands on her hips and called out boldly, 'I said out. Now!'

There was a movement, a flash of something coming towards her, trying to get past her. She reached out, and her hand grabbed a shoulder. Someone her own height? Her own age? That made her even bolder – blinking angry, in fact. Someone her own age trying to hitch a free ride, and getting her into trouble! No way! She clung on to the shoulder, swung her fist, caught a cheek with her blow. She was a good fighter. But a second later she was punched right back. She staggered, but didn't let go, and pulled whoever was there right down with her. She fell back over the coffin, him with her. Him! It was a boy. That made her madder still. She began punching wildly. So did he. 'You pig!' she yelled. 'If you've broken anything in here, I'll kill you!'

The boy let out a yell of his own. He pushed himself away from her. 'You're a girl!'

'Don't let that stop you!' She whacked him again. This time he didn't hit back. What did he think he was? Some kind of gentleman? 'What are you doing here?'

She could certainly land a punch. I sat back, felt my jaw. I couldn't be blamed for not realising she was a girl. She was wearing jeans and an old jacket and her hair was short and wild looking. She had a headful of dark curls that looked like an untamed jungle. And boy, was she strong.

'What are you doing here?' she asked again.

'I hitched a lift. Sorry. I was a bit desperate.' I pointed at the coffin, picked up the head again. 'What on earth is all this?'

She snatched the head from me, held it against her as if it was the family pet. 'It's for the fair. We want to vamp up the ghost train – one of our other rides isn't working and . . . What am I telling you all this for? It's none of your business.'

'I got the fright of my life, thought I was travelling with a vampire.'

She stood up and carried the head over to a box at the side. I saw then it was filled with pieces of very real-looking disembodied corpses. She began tightening ropes around the monster face. 'Come on, make yourself useful,' she ordered. 'Help me with this coffin.'

I stood back, wondering what on earth she wanted me to do. She glared at me. 'It needs tying up. Here.'

She began to push the coffin back against the side. I bent to help her. It wasn't that heavy, but in spite of everything the thought of it made me smile. What had I got myself into now?

She glared at me. 'What's so funny?'

I didn't get a chance to answer.

'Shanti! Are you in there?' It was a man's voice. He was heading our way.

This Shanti – funny name, I thought – looked alarmed. She called back. 'Yeah, Uncle Ben.' Then she looked at me. 'You can't be found here.' Her eyes searched round for somewhere for me to hide.

'Behind the tarpaulin,' I said, pulling it across. 'I can hide there.'

She shook her head and her wild hair wobbled. 'No, he'll lift that out first.' Her eyes roamed the truck, settled on the coffin. 'In there.'

'No way! There's already a skeleton in there.'

She snapped open the lid. The skeleton sat up again, almost as if he was daring me to join him. 'Bags of room for you both.'

'Shanti!' This Uncle Ben was getting closer, walking around the outside of the truck.

'If my uncle finds you here, he'll call the police.'

Should I be afraid of that any more? I could tell them I was the boy who warned them about Jane Faulkner. I would be safe at last.

Or would I? The Dark Men were everywhere. What if instead of taking me to a police station, I was led back to the Dark Man, and the assassin, Salou?

No. Couldn't risk that. Not yet.

'Shanti!' Her uncle, just a step away.

'Take your pick,' she said. 'My uncle Ben . . . or the coffin?'

24

'Everything's secure, Uncle Ben.' The girl, this Shanti, sounded tense, as if she expected Uncle Ben to shout at her.

Uncle Ben, when he answered, snapped the words out. 'Better be.' His voice was gruff. 'Barry said things were moving about.'

'Don't listen to him. It's his driving. It's a wonder there's anything left in one piece. Anyway, a bomb could go off and he wouldn't hear it. He's always listening to that loud music of his. Feel these ropes.'

I felt the whole truck shudder as he jumped into the back.

'There. Couldn't get them any tighter,' Shanti said.

'I've already got one ride not working . . . I don't want anything to happen to this one.'

'Have they turned up to dismantle it yet?'

You could tell by his mood that somebody hadn't turned up. 'No. I've been waiting here all day. I can't get them on the phone. I've kept the fair closed for nothing!'

'Never mind, Uncle Ben. It'll be a great night. The fair'll be jam-packed with punters when we do open.

And at least it's not raining.' She was eager to please him. Too eager.

Uncle Ben only grunted. 'OK, we'll have to start getting this lot unloaded.'

I had hoped then he would get out of the truck, give me a chance to run. No such luck.

'I'll help,' Shanti said.

'You go and see to your aunt.'

'I'll help with this first.'

He cut her off. 'Get Barry to come and help me. You go to your aunt. She's been asking for you.'

Don't leave me! I felt like shouting it. It didn't matter that I knew the skeleton lying beside me was man-made. It was the very fact that I was shut in a coffin that was giving me the creeps. Why didn't I just leap up and frighten the life out of him, take him so much by surprise he couldn't stop me pushing past him, escaping?

Why couldn't I do that?

And I knew why. Something told me the girl would be in a lot of trouble if her uncle found out I was in there. She would get the blame. The eagerness to please him I heard in her voice, the panic to hide me as soon as she heard him call out – could I really drop her in it?

But why should I care?

And yet I did.

People mattered.

No one was expendable. Ryan had thought that some people were, so had his dad – and then I could hear the Dark Man saying it, and someone else agreeing with him, someone I was afraid of. I knew I didn't like this someone. I couldn't see him – only heard the word *expendable*.

I began to sweat, though the afternoon was icy cold. I was sweating as I remembered that someone from my past, someone I hated.

Who knows what else I might have remembered lying there in that dark, enclosed space? It was as if my whole memory was trying to break through that one small crack.

But it was all gone in a split second.

I felt the coffin being lifted. The skeleton bumped against me.

The crack in my memory closed.

25

'What have you got in here? Gold bars?' It was another man's voice I heard, not Uncle Ben's. A younger man. Could it be this Barry? The coffin was being lifted roughly from the back of the truck.

It was Uncle Ben who answered. 'Just get on with it, Barry. I want to open up at five.'

'Suits me,' Barry said. 'I've got a date.' He seemed to be waiting for Uncle Ben to ask more, but he didn't. 'You did remember it's my night off?' No answer. 'Driving these things about gives me the creeps. Coffins, ghost trains, half-eaten corpses. First time I've transported a skeleton.' He was laughing, but if he expected a jovial response, he was talking to the wrong guy.

The coffin was dumped on to the ground with such a thud I was amazed the lid didn't fly open and me and my pal the skeleton shoot up. Boy, poor Barry really would need clean underpants then.

'Grab it properly! That cost me a fortune!' Uncle Ben shouted.

'OK, OK,' Barry moaned. 'It slipped. Give me a chance. Want me to check the skeleton's still in one piece?'

I held my breath. That was all I needed. But Uncle Ben was having none of it.

'Get a move on. Stop wasting time.'

I heard Barry mutter something under his breath. I think he was swearing. Then I was being carried roughly by both of them, in silence. Where was I being taken now?

That question was answered a second later.

'Where do want it?' Barry asked.

'Let's take it straight into the ghost train. It needs to be set up for when we open,' Uncle Ben answered.

Inside the ghost train! How did I ever get into these things?

Shanti watched her uncle and Barry carry the coffin from the truck, watched to see exactly where they would lay it down. She'd hoped perhaps they would leave it somewhere, behind one of the caravans or stalls maybe, so she could run out later and set the boy free. She watched in dismay as they carried the coffin straight into the back entrance of the ghost train. Now she would have to get in there, get him out of the coffin and out of the ghost train without anybody spotting him. Her responsibility. She sighed. She sometimes felt everything was her responsibility.

Who was he? He looked like a tramp. His hair was wild and dark, and his clothes, creased and dirty. His green jacket was badly torn at the sleeve. He looked as if no one cared about him at all.

No time to think about that boy. Not yet. Her first

priority was to see to her aunt. Shanti knew she hadn't been asking for her. Aunt Serena was well aware that Shanti had been sent off with Barry and would be gone most of the day. She never asked for anyone, never caused anyone any trouble, not Aunt Serena. There was always a smile in her eyes when she saw Shanti. And Shanti did everything she could for her aunt – made her as comfortable as she was able. A caravan life was hard for Aunt Serena, travelling from one town to another. Doctors were always advising a hospice, but she wouldn't hear of it. She'd lived all her life in a caravan, she would die in one, she said.

Shanti couldn't bear to think of her aunt dying. She wanted her to live. Not only because she loved her, but also because she was sure Uncle Ben wouldn't keep her around if anything happened to Aunt Serena. He'd told her so many times, always out of her aunt's hearing, that she'd be sent back . . . and there was no one, nothing to go back to.

'Shanti . . .' Her aunt murmured her name as she stepped inside the dimly lit caravan. Shanti hurried into the bedroom, sat beside her on the bed and clasped her hand. 'Glad you're back.' She took a long time over her words. 'You shouldn't have gone. Too young.'

That was what Barry had said too. Too young. But Uncle Ben couldn't go. He'd been waiting for the people from the company they'd hired the roller coaster from. They were supposed to be sending men to dismantle it, and because of that the fair wasn't opening till five – late for a Sunday, especially with so much going on in the town. For starters, there was this water festival – the docks were full of boats, submarines, tall ships and steamers. Lots of people were expected at the fair – and money was being lost because they were closed. It didn't help that there was never enough staff. No wonder Uncle Ben was in a foul mood.

So Shanti had insisted she'd go instead. She was trying to make herself indispensable. That was the word – *indispensable*.

And then her thoughts went back to the boy in the coffin – yet another problem. She had to get that boy away before her uncle found him.

26

I waited till all was quiet. I had heard Uncle Ben grunt something to Barry, heard their footsteps fade. Still I waited – I needed to be sure it was safe to move.

Even though I wanted to scream and yell and kick, I waited.

I had to get out of there.

Already the feeling of darkness closing in, walls closing in, was making it difficult for me to breathe. I pushed at the lid. It stayed shut.

I took a deep breath, pushed again, harder this time. It was only a joke coffin, I kept telling myself, not a real one, not sealed tight, not screwed down. Not six feet underground.

I pushed again. It had to open.

But it didn't.

I lifted my feet and kicked. The skeleton beside me seemed to snuggle closer. *He's not real.* I kept repeating that over and over. *He's not real. Nothing here is real.*

The coffin stayed shut. I was locked in. Tremors ran through my body. My bones quivered. *Help me!*

No one to help me. There was never anyone to help me.

My life seemed to be filled with death.

And there in the darkness, afraid and alone, one hand was held out to me; one face seemed to appear in front of me.

And it was the face of the Dark Man.

My only friend. My protector.

Why was I running from him? He would get me out of there.

And for a moment, for a split second, I trusted him.

Whispers in a dark place. Something coming. Something terrible. Something to change the world.

And the Dark Man would protect me.

Why were my memories of him so mixed up?

But even as I thought it the image of him changed. The light became shadow. His face became as skeletal as the one beside me, only way more frightening because he was real.

The Dark Man is your enemy! Don't forget that, Ram, I told myself.

I had to get out of there! I beat at the lid with my fists, but I knew no one was there.

No one was ever there for me.

The girl had forgotten me.

The Dark Man was my enemy, not my protector.

I was alone. Always alone.

Locked in this dark place for ever.

27

Shanti knew Uncle Ben wouldn't waste any more time. Nothing was going to stop him opening at five. Soon the fairground would come to life, rides open up, all the stalls uncovered. People would begin to flood over the bridge from the other side of the docks. Now was her chance.

Her uncle was too busy to notice what she was doing. She saw him from the window of the caravan, his face like thunder, checking the fencing around the broken ride. Having to close that ride down yesterday had made him so angry. But it had been erected too close to the edge of the dock, he insisted. It wasn't safe. And Uncle Ben was a real stickler for safety.

She tiptoed out of the bedroom. Her aunt was asleep. Shanti kept thinking of the boy in the coffin. She had a sudden horrified thought. Goodness! Did he have enough air in there? She hadn't even considered that. Maybe he was dead already. That was all she needed, a dead boy in a coffin . . . How would she ever explain that? Maybe she shouldn't have locked it from the outside. But she'd been so afraid it would open accidentally with all the lifting and carrying, and he would have been found.

Oh, why were these things always happening to her?

She drew back the curtain at the window and looked out again. Her uncle was still busy, striding around the stalls, checking that everything was in order before officially opening the fair. She had to get the boy out of that coffin before the ghost train was in operation.

Uncle Ben was too busy to bother with Shanti. She slipped quietly from the caravan, doing her best not to disturb her aunt.

The fairground was coming alive. There was a wonderful holiday atmosphere in the town, what with the water festival on the docks and the peace marchers camping out in the square on the other side of the bridge. There were jugglers and acrobats too. Every spare space was taken up with someone putting on a show. Later there would be fireworks.

That was what the fair brought to each town they visited, Shanti thought – a holiday atmosphere. This was home to Shanti, had been for a long time, and she loved it. She loved the atmosphere and the life, loved travelling from place to place, meeting new people all the time. Interesting people, strange people, sometimes weird people.

That reminded her again of the boy in the coffin. There was something weird about him.

Yet she always had the fear that her uncle would send her back, first chance he got, to the place she'd been before. She couldn't remember where that place was, just that something bad had happened there. If her aunt died, he might just do that. She wouldn't be indispensable any more.

Barry and some of the other men were trying to fit the open-mouth facade of the new entrance to the ghost train into place. There was no time to lose. They didn't notice her as she crept round the back. She knew exactly how to sneak inside so that nobody could see her.

She found the door, pulled back the black curtains and stepped into darkness.

The dark didn't bother Shanti. She knew the horrors in there were plasterboard and fake. The coffin was lying near the tracks, on its own. The dim light above it was off for the moment. When the ride started and the carriages came past, the light would switch on, the coffin lid would open and the skeleton would sit up – the cue for other horrors to emerge from the fake rocks: half-eaten corpses, cannibal zombies, axe murderers. Everyone loved the ghost train.

Shanti crouched down and put her ear to the top of the coffin. She heard nothing.

She tapped gently, spoke softly. 'Are you still in there?'

There was a growl. 'There isn't anywhere else for me to go, is there? Get me out of here!'

He began banging on the lid.

'Shut up!' Shanti's voice was still soft. 'Someone will hear you.'

There was a quiver of panic in his answer. But he didn't shout. 'Get me out of here *now*!'

Her hands were sweating as she fumbled with the catch. The lid sprung open. Boy and skeleton shot up. It was a contest as to which one looked whiter. The boy dived out of the coffin, and she could hear his panicked breathing as he crouched on all fours, drawing in great lungfuls of air.

'I'm sorry,' she said. 'I locked it. I thought it might just open if I didn't.'

She expected an argument, but to her surprise he waved her explanation away. 'I understand,' he said.

He looked around him. The top half of a corpse was hidden in the space beside him. Beyond that, there were more crouching corpses ready to crawl out. 'Where the hell am I?'

'You're inside the ghost train, where else?'

He almost smiled. 'Couldn't be any crazier than the other places I've been today.'

She knelt beside him. 'Are you lost? Have you run away? Who are you?'

He sat back. She could see pearls of sweat drip from under his dark hair. He wiped them away with his sleeve. 'Wish I knew,' he said.

28

I was still shaking. Locked in that coffin for so long, all kinds of fears had gripped me, fears I couldn't hold down. The fear that I would never get out, that I would be trapped in that dark, tight space for ever.

Had to stop thinking about that. *Get a grip, Ram*, I thought.

'Where is this place?'

'It's called Greenock,' the girl said. 'We're here because there's a big water festival on in the town and there are so many people around. That's also because of that big conference going on close by. There's going to be a huge peace march tomorrow.'

I stood up. 'I have to get out of here.'

'Good. I want rid of you as well.'

'Thanks.'

'What did you mean, you wish you knew who you were?'

Her face was grimy, this Shanti, her dark hair wild and curly. She looked as much of a runaway as I did.

'I've lost my memory.' I told her. 'Haven't a clue who I am, where I came from. Nothing.'

'Since when?' She didn't sound as if she believed me.

What could I tell her? Since I'd woken up in the stairwell of a tower block, found a dying man, been accused of his murder and then pursued by the real killer. It hadn't stopped since then.

'Someone's after me,' was enough to tell her. 'I call him the Dark Man.'

'Why? Why do you call him the Dark Man?'

It occurred to me for the first time that I didn't know why I called him that, why I always had. Something tugged at my memory again, something about dark . . . dark . . . dark conspiracies. I felt her shaking me.

'Are you OK? You looked vacant there. Maybe you always look like that. I knew there was something weird about you.' She tutted. 'I've picked up a nutter.'

I tried to get back the thought of these dark conspiracies, but the memory – had it been a memory? – it was all gone.

'I'm not a nutter!' I said. 'I'm telling you the truth. I keep remembering bits of my past, but never the whole thing. Little things keep coming back to me, but not enough, and I have so little time. I need to remember soon.'

'What's your hurry?'

It all began to tumble out. Maybe I needed someone to talk to. I found myself telling her everything – about the Dark Man, and the secret I had locked in my memory. I told her too all that had happened today. How I'd met the man I thought was Emir Khan at the railway station, about the explosion, how we'd run, and then my discovery that this Emir Khan wasn't who he said he was . . .

'Emir Khan? There was a newsflash on the truck radio. They found his body in a flat in Glasgow . . . Wait a minute . . .' Her eyes went wide. '*You* were at that explosion today at the train station?' Her hands flew to her mouth with excitement. 'They're talking about some mystery boy who was there, saving people . . . and then he just disappeared. Was that you?'

I grinned. 'I think it might have been. But there's no mystery. Just had to get out of there quick. I'm not a ghost.'

'Wow!' She seemed well impressed. 'Why don't you just go to the police? Tell them you're the boy from the station. They could help you. They might even give you a medal.'

'I can't go to the police. I don't know who to trust. Even if I did, they wouldn't believe what I really have to tell them.'

And yet I remembered the voice on the phone, the man called John Julian. I could trust him, surely? He had no links with the Dark Man.

'What have you got to tell them?'

'That something's going to happen tomorrow . . . something big. I just don't know what it is, or where it's going to happen. It's all locked in here! I can't remember.'

'Why don't you just tell them that – they can look into it?'

'There isn't time. And the Dark Man works for the government. There's some kind of conspiracy and he's part of it . . . I don't trust anybody. I can't.'

'Does this Dark Man know you're here?'

I heard the worry in her voice. She didn't want him anywhere near here.

'No, but he went in this direction. I wanted to follow him.'

'Where did you get into the truck?'

'At a motel. You were coming out of the petrol station.'

'We didn't stay on the motorway. There's a big diversion so no one goes near Hanover House. Your Dark Man could be anywhere.'

'Hanover House?'

'It's the big estate up the road where the conference is being held.' She moved to the exit. 'Look, you better just leave now.'

Dying to be rid of me, I thought. 'Why are you so afraid of your uncle?' I asked her.

'I'm not afraid of him . . .'

'Well, you're certainly trying to please him a lot.'

'He's not really my uncle. They adopted me – well, Aunt Serena did. I don't think Uncle Ben was ever keen on the idea. I don't know who my real family are.'

'Have you asked them?'

'She's always said she'll tell me one day. I can't keep asking. Aunt Serena's dying. My uncle's always busy. I don't want to hurt them.'

Poor girl. It seemed she had almost as many problems as I did. 'I'm sorry about this,' I said. 'I'll move on.'

'I can't help. You see that, don't you?' She still wasn't sure whether to believe me or not. I could have been making it all up – she hoped I was. 'Are you hungry?'

All day people had been asking me that. I hadn't had anything to eat yet. 'I'm absolutely starving.'

She seemed to come to a decision. 'OK, wait here. I'll see what I can do. And then you've got to move on, OK?' She hurried to the back and lifted the black curtain. 'By the way, what's your name?'

I shrugged. 'Don't know . . . but I call myself Ram.'

29

5 P.M.

It was too dark inside the ghost train. Even though my common sense told me nothing there could hurt me, I'd had enough of the dark, enough of coffins and skeletons and ghosts. I crossed to the back and lifted aside the black curtain, opened the door just a crack to let a bit of the fairground light come in. It was almost dark again.

There were no people passing behind the ride, no one to notice me. I could hear the sound of tarpaulins snapping in the breeze, the calls as stalls were opened up. I pictured the hoopla stalls and the rifle stalls – stalls where you could win a cuddly toy or a goldfish. Seagulls squawked in the sky as they flapped above the fair, which had been set up next to the river on the docks, and I could see between the caravans and stalls across a bridge and beyond that the white top of a big marquee. I could even make out the masts of the tall ships, quivering against the clouds.

There was another silhouette: a roller coaster, a sprawling tower of steel that curved and looped and swooped against the sky. It seemed to be teetering dangerously close to the edge of the dock, almost as if one tip of a finger would send it plummeting into the deep water.

I thought of that policeman again. Detective Inspector John Julian. He sounded gruff, but dependable. And he wasn't one of the Dark Men, I was sure of that.

Had I at least protected Jane Faulkner? Why did I even care? I didn't know the woman, had never met her. Yet it felt important to some part of me that she *was* safe.

From here, behind the door, I could see the caravans. Some of them were in darkness. Others were ablaze with lights. Doors were lying open, people coming and going. One of the caravans stood on its own away behind the others. Could that be Shanti's caravan? There was a single light in one of the windows, a warm glow from a bedroom maybe. Her aunt was dying, Shanti had said. Was she dying now?

I shook away these dark thoughts. Dark thoughts all around me. What was I doing here? There was something I had to stop, something that was going to happen tomorrow, and I still didn't know what it was or how to stop it. I pulled the door closed.

I was in the dark again, in more ways than one.

30

Shanti tried to be as quiet as possible as she went about the kitchen gathering food for the boy . . . Ram, he had called himself. He was a strange one, she thought. Could his story be true? And could he really be this mystery boy she had heard them talking about on the radio?

She didn't even switch on the light in the kitchen. She had enough light from the glow of the lamp that streamed through the open door from her aunt's bedroom. Her aunt was sleeping, she was certain of it, so she didn't want to wake her. She just wanted rid of that boy. Ram. She didn't want him bringing any Dark Man, or any other trouble to the carnival. And that boy was trouble. She had enough of the gypsy in her to believe her feelings, her instincts. He was big trouble, and she had brought him here. It was all her fault.

She had slipped off her shoes and walked about on tiptoe – learned long ago how to be quiet for her aunt's sake.

Some chicken – she took it out of the fridge – some bread too, and a couple of cans of Coke. All the time she was waiting, listening, for a movement from the bedroom, or for the sound of this Dark Man. The boy had made him seem so real, she imagined she could see him stalking the fairground already, searching for the boy. The picture was so clear in her head she was almost sure that if she looked out of the window, he would be there, in shadow, watching her.

Or . . . was she seeing some part of the future?

Her aunt had told her that if she opened her mind the gift would come – the gift of second sight. It was lying dormant within her, Aunt Serena said.

Shanti wasn't so sure. She had had no sign of it up to now and didn't know what to expect when it did come. A vision of the future? A vivid picture in her mind? Or just a feeling, an instinct? Or was it different for everyone? How would she know the difference between instincts, gut feelings, and the gift?

There was a sound from the bedroom, her aunt turning in her bed. Shanti stiffened, waiting for her to call. She would want a drink, or perhaps need to get up for the toilet. But when she called out to her softly, it wasn't anything like what Shanti was expecting.

'Shanti?' Her aunt's voice was no more than a whisper. 'Shanti . . . who's the boy?'

I leapt to my feet when I heard the door being pulled open and the black curtain swept across. I slid behind one of the papier mâché rocks and crouched down among the rotting corpses of the never-been-alive dead. I heaved a sigh of relief when I saw it was Shanti.

She had a coat wrapped round her, and her dark eyes darted to the left and the right as if she was sure her uncle would suddenly appear. 'Come with me,' she said.

'Come with you? I thought you were bringing me food. You want me out of here, remember?'

Her bright eyes sparked with fire. 'I do, don't doubt it. But the ghost train will be switched on soon and the punters might get a real fright if they see you.'

'Just give me some food. I'll be on my way.'

Shanti gripped my sleeve as if I was trying to leave that second. 'No. You're coming to our caravan. My aunt wants to see you.'

I pulled away from her. 'You told your aunt about me!'

'I didn't have to,' she said, still hauling me on. 'Aunt Serena has the gift. She knows you're here. She senses you.'

I didn't believe her. She'd said I was a nutter. I thought she was the one who was the nutter. She'd told her aunt about me and now she was trying to cover it up. I wanted to run.

So why didn't I pull away and do just that? Instead, I let her lead me from the back exit of the ghost train towards her aunt's caravan.

It *was* the one that sat at the furthest edge of the fairground, tucked away. So perhaps the noise, the bustle, would be diminished there. Shanti had said her uncle didn't care about anyone, but he cared enough to make sure his wife's caravan was as far from the noise of the fair as possible. That solitary glow of light in one of the windows was warm, golden, welcoming. Her aunt was waiting for me – a sick old woman, bedridden. I could run any time I wanted. She was no threat to me.

I was intrigued. Why did she want to see me?

We darted between caravans and wires and pipes. The fair was busy now. Rides were lit up and the air was filled with the sounds of fairground music. Already I could smell burgers and doughnuts and toffee apples. I looked up again at that roller coaster rising high in the sky. It was the only ride that was still in darkness.

'What's wrong with that one?' I asked, pointing.

'Don't even ask. That's why my uncle's in such a bad mood. He paid a lot of money to hire that ride, but he doesn't think it's safe. They were supposed to send people to dismantle it today, but they didn't turn up. I wouldn't like to be them when they do. We could have been making a lot of money out of that.'

'Why? What's so special about it?'

And her answer sent a shiver all through me, and I didn't know why. 'It's supposed to take you places you've never been,' she said. 'It's called the Ride of Death.'

31

The caravan was warm and cosy. Shanti told me to sit on a sofa while she went in to see her aunt. She closed the door to the bedroom behind her, but I had a glimpse of white covers on the bed and a pale figure lying there. My mouth was dry and my heart was racing. I had no time to sit waiting to talk with a dying old woman.

I picked up an evening newspaper that was lying on the table. My hands were shaking so much the paper trembled. No wonder after the day I'd had . . . and it wasn't over yet.

The front page was almost completely taken up with the explosion this morning.

Only this morning? It seemed days back.

But the headlines were shared with another story. That politician's missing daughter, kidnapped, and the ransom demand –

FREE THEM OR SHE DIES

– was the graphic headline.

And underneath that, a quote from the politician: *'She may be wild, but she's always been my little treasure,'*

Angus Lennox said today.

Something stirred in my memory, but I had no time to think about it because then I saw the photograph of Sapphire Lennox taken the day before she'd been reported missing.

She looked totally different from the girl I'd seen on television earlier. She'd completely changed her image and her hair colour. Gone were the blonde curls. Now her hair was raven black and it hung long over her face, hiding one eye. And she was wearing a white dress.

I felt the hairs on the back of my neck rise.

I had seen this girl before. But the dress had been dirty. The raven hair had hung wild, covering her face, making it appear that she had no eyes.

The ghost in the graveyard.

The missing girl.

Sapphire Lennox.

'My aunt's ordered me to give you something to eat first,' Shanti said as she came out of the bedroom, closing the door quietly behind her.

'Shanti . . .' The paper still shook in my hand as I held it out to her. 'I've seen this Sapphire Lennox. And I think she's dead. Last night, I think I saw the ghost of this girl in a graveyard.'

Shanti snatched the paper from my hand. There was a photo of the politician too, with his daughter. His arm was round her waist. They both looked happy. I felt sick. He was hoping he would get his daughter back alive, unaware that she was already dead.

Shanti didn't look impressed. 'Oh yeah. You've only just got here, you've not even met Aunt Serena . . . and suddenly, you've got the gift.'

I had expected her to be intrigued, at least. But not this. 'What's your problem?'

She slammed some chicken between two slices of bread and pushed it at me. 'You don't understand.' She opened a bottle of Coke. 'Aunt Serena adopted me because my mother was a traveller too. Fair folk . . . at least, that's what Aunt Serena's always said. When Uncle Ben's got a little drink in him, he sometimes says I don't belong here. But my aunt believes that somewhere deep down I have the gift. The gift of second sight.' She sat beside me on the sofa, shook her head. 'But I haven't. I've tried and I've tried, but nothing ever comes. And when Aunt Serena dies . . . he won't keep me here.'

'Would that be so bad?'

Wrong thing to say.

'The worst thing I can imagine! I love it here, love everything about the fair – the rides, the stalls and the people. Sometimes, when there's a big festival on, we set up marquees and we have magicians, conjurors, illusionists.' She said the words as if she loved rolling them about on her tongue. 'I love watching how they make their magic work – sleight of hand, misdirection, making the audience look at one hand when the real magic is happening in the other. I couldn't bear ever to leave here.'

I could see there was a fire in her when she spoke about it.

'Hasn't your aunt told you where you came from, who you are?'

'She always said she would tell me everything when I was older.'

'Why don't you ask her again . . . before she . . .'

'Before she dies? What am I supposed to say? By the way, before you kick the bucket I want a complete rundown of my history.' She looked grim.

'Maybe it doesn't matter who you used to be, where you came from. Maybe not knowing gives you a fresh start. You can be the person you always wanted to be.'

I didn't believe that even as I said it, and neither did Shanti.

'I have to know,' she said.

And I understood that. 'So do I.'

She sighed. 'Then you come along and right off say you have the gift.'

Why wouldn't she listen?

'I haven't got any gift. I'm only saying I've seen her . . . this girl . . . last night in an old deserted graveyard. She's dead. And they don't know it.'

'What makes you think she was a ghost?'

'You didn't see her, Shanti. I was so scared. She was coming right at me . . . floating towards me across this old graveyard.' I shivered again even thinking about it.

She dismissed that. 'You imagined it. Stuck in a graveyard in the middle of the night, you could imagine anything. And then you read this story . . . see this photograph . . . and it reminds you of her. A girl in a white dress. It's all logical. Nothing mysterious at all.' When she explained it like that, it sounded so obvious.

My imagination was going haywire. I didn't believe in ghosts.

Or maybe, I thought, it was because Shanti wasn't going to believe I had seen a ghost until she'd seen one herself.

She stood up. 'Right. If you're finished spluttering crumbs all over the carpet, Aunt Serena will see you now.'

32

5.30 P.M.

Aunt Serena lay back against the pillows, her face as pale as the sheets. She wasn't half as old as I expected, not an old woman at all. Her hair, fanned out on the pillow, was long and dark, and her eyes were the greenest I had ever seen. She didn't take them off me as I walked slowly towards her. I couldn't hold her stare. I glanced around the small room, into its gloomy corners. There wasn't much space for a big man like Uncle Ben.

'My husband sleeps in another caravan,' she said. Her voice was soft.

Had she been reading my mind, I wondered, or had my thoughts just been so obvious?

'He doesn't like sick people.' Shanti couldn't keep the bitterness out of her voice.

'Sit down,' Serena said, patting the bed beside her. 'Have you had something to eat?'

'Shanti's been very kind.' I hoped she knew I was being sarcastic.

'Are you warm enough?'

The cold I always felt in my bones was leaving me,

soaking away in the warmth of the small room. I felt myself relax. The golden glow of the lamp, the cosiness of the caravan and, most of all, Serena's soft, almost hypnotic voice, were giving me a sense of peace.

Not a good thing. I had to be alert. Couldn't afford to relax for a moment.

Serena must have felt me stiffen. She touched my hand. 'Don't worry. Danger's coming, but we have time to talk.'

JJ was back at the hospital. He wanted to make sure Jane Faulkner was still all right. He could have called and asked, but he had wanted to see her for himself, see those brown eyes again.

The nursing staff in the ward couldn't hide their smiles. His own people had been talking. Gruff JJ was getting sentimental. They weren't used to him being so soft. Neither was he. But he had such a strong feeling that he had to keep her safe.

A WPC was by her bed when he entered her room. He thought Jane was sleeping at first, but, as if she could sense him there, her eyes opened and she smiled at him. The WPC noticed and glanced round. She couldn't miss the smile he flashed back at Jane, though he had tried hard to keep his face impassive. She looked away again quickly, probably scared he would reprimand her, but as she turned he saw the corner of her mouth curve into a smile too.

'Is everything all right?' Jane whispered.

'Everything's fine,' he said.

His superiors were delighted. Getting Salou had been a coup. They would have preferred him alive, but at least dead, he could harm no one again. This was a victory, but a small one. JJ knew that Salou was a part of something much, much bigger; they'd only hit the tip of the iceberg.

He had a sinking feeling deep in his stomach.

'You've lost your memory,' Serena said.

'How did you know that?'

She managed a smile. 'Nothing supernatural, don't worry.' Her eyes moved to Shanti sitting on the other side of the bed. 'Shanti told me.'

'What else did she tell you?'

Her voice was so soft I had to edge closer to hear her. It was as if she had to summon up all her strength to speak. 'That someone is after you. You call him the Dark Man, and you think you have a terrible secret locked in your head.'

'Seems she only missed out my shoe size and you would know everything I know about me.'

Shanti said, 'Would have told her if I'd known it.'

Serena's hand reached out again to mine. I took it – didn't feel in the least embarrassed holding her hand. She really did have a peaceful, relaxing effect on me, even though there was no warmth in the bony hand, as if it was dead already. As if death was slowly making its way from her hands to the rest of her body.

'Would you like me to try to help you remember?'

The silence seemed to grow thick in the room. I

115

couldn't answer for what seemed an age. 'You could do that?' I whispered.

It was Shanti who answered. 'Among Aunt Serena's many accomplishments, she's also a hypnotist.'

'You can hypnotise me? Maybe bring my memory back?' I shook my head. Hypnotism – that would mean I would not be in control of my own body. I didn't like the sound of that. What if I lost what little memory I had?

'Don't be afraid. You need someone to unlock what's in your mind. I might be able to help you. And at some level you will know what's happening, I promise.'

Why should I believe this woman? I'd only just met her. Why *did* I believe this woman? Because, oddly, I found that I did, in spite of the number of times I'd been let down.

Serena leant back on the pillows, closed her eyes. I thought for a moment she was about to die. Even Shanti shot from her seat on the other side of the bed. 'Are you sure you're up to this?'

'I have to be,' she said. 'Because time is running out. He has to piece things together. Something tells me it's vital he remembers, and if I can help . . . I must.'

33

The room was quiet, middle-of-the-night kind of quiet, even though the night had barely begun. Outside I could hear people shouting, children giggling, music booming; the funfair had come alive. But all of that seemed a million miles in the distance. Serena's voice began to murmur. She still held my hand. I felt at peace.

I closed my eyes.

I would be alert at some level, she had said, no matter how relaxed I was, and I felt better about that. I didn't want to lose control in front of these people I hardly knew. I didn't want to come out of this and know nothing of what had happened.

'I want you to imagine yourself floating up and up, beyond the clouds, beyond the stars, into eternal space.'

At first I thought I'd never be able to do that. Nothing could shut out the knowledge that I was here in this caravan, with a fairground outside.

And yet, as I listened to Serena's soft voice I felt myself become weightless as gossamer, blown like a feather in a breeze, up and up, until I was hovering above the caravans. I saw the fairground below me, moving further and further into the distance. Higher and higher I floated, until the earth itself was only a speck in dark space.

'What is your name?' Her soft voice seemed to float beside me.

I tried to think. Names. Names I could relate to. Robert, Thomas, Simon . . . nothing stirred my memory. 'I don't know,' I heard a voice saying. Was it mine? 'I call myself Ram.'

'Why?' she asked me.

I tried to think. I really tried to push open that closed door in my mind.

'Because it's important. Ram is important. It's from my past, and it means something.'

And it was. That was the reason I had chosen the name. Not a random choice. Something from my past I needed to remember . . . but what?

Her soft voice spoke again. 'Don't worry. That will come. Tell me what you *do* remember.'

I didn't feel as if I was being hypnotised. I was still floating high above. Her voice was so gentle it seemed to be coming from somewhere in a dream. She was taking me back to the only thing I did remember.

'I was running,' I said. 'It was dark . . . I was in some dark tunnel . . .'

And suddenly I was there, watching it all happen. An observer in my own past. I could see myself running towards the light and there was someone behind me. A voice called out, *'Run! Time's running out. It's up to you!'*

Why couldn't I see who that someone was? I wanted so badly for it to be my dad, but I was afraid. There was a flicker of a memory I couldn't catch.

'What are you supposed to stop?'

'Some terrible disaster. Something awful that's going to happen. Now I know it's going to happen tomorrow. I promised I would stop it.'

'Who did you promise?'

A flicker again, in and out of my mind in an instant.

I was breathing hard, watching myself still running. Serena gently squeezed my hand.

'I don't know – the person running after me in the tunnel, I guess . . .'

'Who is that? I want you to imagine yourself turning round, turning to face him, to look at him . . . Who is he?'

I knew I didn't want to see, that some part of me didn't want to remember this. Yet I tried to do what she said, tried to make the boy I was watching from above turn round. It was as if I was directing a film. The actors would do my bidding.

'Turn round.' Did I say it aloud? 'Turn round to face him. You want to see his face. Turn around . . . I can see him,' I said. And I was no longer floating. I was there, back in that tunnel. He was standing in front of me. I saw his face at last.

I felt as if I was falling into a black hole. Because I knew that face, knew that man. Not my dad.

The Lone Bomber.

And I knew in that second why the memory was so clear. I *had* been there in that underground car park. And I knew why I had been there.

'I was trying to stop him.' The words tumbled out. 'I was trying to stop him from planting the bomb.'

My mind felt like a boat tossing in a stormy sea. I was trying to steer it into calm waters so I could think straight.

'*Time's running out. It's up to you.*' So what did those words mean? Who had said them?

Couldn't have been him. Not him – trying to plant a bomb. No. It must have been me, telling myself, thinking aloud . . .

I was so confused, so unsure of what was real.

Serena's voice broke into my thoughts. 'How did you know he was going to plant the bomb?'

Another question I couldn't answer. Or could I? All at once I reached calm waters. It came to me that I *did* know. I could be sure of something. 'Because I know all about this conspiracy. I know everything. That's why he's after me, the Dark Man. I can stop it . . . but I don't know how. I'm only a boy. I'm only a boy!'

I was growing agitated. I didn't want to remember any more. There was something even more terrifying trying to surface in my memory, something I didn't want to face. I was too scared, too scared to remember it all.

I snapped my eyes open. 'I've had enough!' I said.

Serena looked exhausted, lying back on her pillows, watching me. 'What is it you don't want to remember?'

'I do want to remember! What makes you think I don't?'

'Don't shout!' Shanti snapped at me.

Had I been shouting? 'I'm sorry,' I said.

Shanti climbed on the other side of the bed, beside her aunt. She felt her brow. 'Are you sure you're all right?'

Her aunt nodded, but Shanti stayed where she was, close to her, stroking her brow gently.

'It's all in there.' Serena tapped my head. 'You only needed the key to unlock it. Tonight, you turned the key. The door's been opened. It won't close now. Bit by bit everything will come back . . .' Then she said something ominous. 'Whether you want it to or not, your memory will trickle through till it becomes a flood and bursts that door wide open.'

She closed her eyes and lay back. Lying there, with her black hair against the white of the pillows, she looked so deathly pale – and somehow familiar. Her eyes opened for a second, focused on me. Then they slowly closed again.

Shanti motioned me out of the room. 'She needs to rest,' she whispered.

Serena touched her hand. 'Not yet,' she said. 'Sit by my bed. Just give me a moment.'

34

6 P.M.

We sat still by her bed while Serena rested. I wanted to
ask if there was anything else they could do for her, but
somehow I already knew the answer. I looked across at
Shanti. Her eyes were filled with tears. I felt sorry for
her.

Her whole life would change when her aunt died, she
said. She might have to leave this place she so clearly
loved.

I wished I could help her, but I had too much on my
mind for the moment. I was still sweating from what I
had seen. I had tried to stop the Lone Bomber from
planting the bomb that day in London. So how had I
ended up in Scotland? Like my name . . . it couldn't have
been a random choice. Something had drawn me here.

Serena opened her eyes.

'You've done enough, Aunty.' Shanti was worried.

Serena waved away her concern. She looked at me.
'What did you remember, Ram?'

'I was there with the Lone Bomber, ' I told her. 'I was
in that explosion. That's probably how I lost my

memory. I was trying to stop him planting the bomb.'

'There's something else you don't want to remember.'

Serena was right. A second more and I would have known what it was, and I knew I couldn't face it. But I shook my head. 'No. You're wrong. I don't remember anything else.' I couldn't admit that I had turned away from something. 'It's the conspiracy. I'll remember what's going to happen tomorrow if I just give myself the chance to think about it.'

In my head I was still running from that tunnel, desperately trying to work things out in my mind.

'I know something big is going to happen. And the Dark Men are behind it all.'

I was shaking as I sat there. I was so close to the truth. Why was I afraid?

'I was in London . . . so how come I ended up here?' That's what I couldn't understand. 'Not just to get as far away as possible. There's another reason.'

'Because . . . whatever is going to happen tomorrow . . . is going to happen here?' Shanti suggested.

'And something *is* going to happen here tomorrow,' Serena reminded her.

'Of course!' said Shanti excitedly. 'There are going to be peace marches across the country, and the biggest one is going from here to Glasgow, and from there they'll meet up with the Edinburgh marchers. They're expecting people in their thousands. That must be it. They're going to target the marchers!'

Could that possibly be the answer? I wondered. But if the marches were happening all over the country, why had I come here? 'There has to be something else I'm missing.' Sleeper cells – I was thinking of the sleeper cells all over the country too. Why did they need sleeper cells if they were going to target the peace marchers?

Shanti was still rattling on. 'Now, if they were going to do something really big, they've missed their chance. They should have done it yesterday when we had the Prime Minister and the US President and all the world leaders just up the road.'

I stared at her in shock. 'What?'

'At the Hanover House estate. That big conference about terrorism and how the world should deal with it. Everyone was here. But the leaders left the house this morning.' It was all I'd been hearing about, all day. Of course. 'So you see they could have bombed Hanover House yesterday and got most of the world leaders. You couldn't get much bigger than that.'

So why hadn't they done that? I wondered. 'Security would probably be too tight.' I was almost talking to myself. 'Wouldn't do them any good. But tomorrow . . . Is there anyone left there?'

'There's still a big meeting going on,' Serena said. 'Deputies, ambassadors, chancellors – lots of top politicians. They're finalising the details, the papers said . . .' She was watching me closely. 'Are you remembering something, Ram?'

'I don't know. There has to be a reason for me coming here, though. It might be to do with these marches, with this conference, but there's something else. I know there has to be something else.'

I was so close to remembering. The answer was trying to push its way into my head. Something about

Hanover House, about the conference. But if this thing was going to happen tomorrow at the marches, I would have to warn someone. Maybe now I had enough information.

I looked at Serena. 'But who do I tell?'

35

I felt useless and helpless. 'Who do I tell?' I asked Serena. 'Who would listen to me?' Because what would happen if they didn't?

'You have to *make* someone listen,' Serena said.

'But how? I'm only a boy.' And suddenly it seemed hopeless. I could never stop it in time.

'You've slipped through their fingers every time. There has to be a reason for that.'

'You have enough information to go to the police,' Shanti added. It was her simple answer. 'You think the peace marches are going to be targeted tomorrow. Or maybe they're still going to blow up Hanover House. They'll have to listen.'

'Yeah, that's really going to work. A boy walks into a police station with information like that. A boy my age, no name, no identity. Yeah, they're really going to listen to me.'

'They'll still have to follow up on it, no matter what age you are. They can't just ignore you,' Shanti said. 'You're warning them about a terrorist plot.'

'First, they'll want to know who I am, who my parents are – want to contact them. And when I tell them I don't know, I can't remember . . . and all I do remember is that I was at the explosion with the Lone Bomber. Oh yes . . . I can see it now. They'll think I'm a headcase.' I felt sick at the thought of it. 'And by the time anyone does take me seriously, it'll be too late.'

'If you don't do something, no one else will,' Serena said.

I turned to her. 'You could tell them. They would listen to you.'

But I could see in that pale face she was too weak to do anything. She shook her head. 'It has to be you,' she whispered.

'But how do I know I won't be telling one of them? One of the Dark Men?' I had put my trust in the man I thought was Emir Khan, hadn't I? And look where it had got me. I had trusted Ryan's dad, and he had been one of them too.

'Isn't there anyone you can trust?' Shanti asked. 'Anyone who might believe you?'

And I remembered John Julian, the policeman I had called earlier today.

Shanti must have read something in my face. 'There is, isn't there?'

There had been nothing on the news of Jane Faulkner being killed. She must surely still be alive . . . Yes, I was sure I could trust this John Julian. I told her quickly who he was. 'I think he would listen to me, but it was just luck I found him before. How do I get in touch with him now? I can't just phone 999 and ask for Detective Inspector John Julian. There's no time . . . so little time.'

'Where was he when you called him before?'

'He was in Emir Khan's flat. It was the only number I knew. I phoned it from that motel I was in. But he wouldn't still be there . . . That was . . .' I thought for a moment. In fact, it had probably only been a few hours ago. 'No, he couldn't still be there.'

Shanti was already hunting in her pockets for her phone. 'It's a crime scene. They're not just going to go away and lock it up for the night. I watch cop shows all the time. There's bound to be some kind of police presence still there. Tell them you called this John Julian before. If he's not there, ask them to put you through to him. Say it's important – a matter of life and death. You can use my phone.'

Could it be as simple as that? One call and a policeman would do the rest?

And could I really trust him?

The voice had been hard as granite. Maybe he too was part of the conspiracy – I had phoned the wrong man, Jane Faulkner was dead, Salou was alive and thriving.

No.

I had to try. If he was one of them, it wouldn't matter after tomorrow anyway.

36

6.15 P.M.

The phone seemed to ring for a long time. For a while I thought Emir Khan's flat must be empty, despite Shanti's cop show expertise. I imagined the sound echoing through dark deserted rooms. Finally, it *was* answered.

'I want to speak to Detective Inspector John Julian. Is he still there . . . ?' My voice trailed away uncertainly. 'I spoke to him earlier.'

I had hoped it would be John Julian who picked up – that, by some miracle, he would still be there and that he would take charge.

But it wasn't John Julian who spoke. It was another, much younger voice. And he wasn't talking to me, not at first. He called to someone else, 'Someone wants to talk to JJ.'

The answer came as clear as if the other man was also on the line. 'Ask them who they are. What do they want?'

'Who are you?' the young policeman asked.

'I spoke to John Julian before . . . I told him about

Jane Faulkner. Is she safe?'

That voice in the background again, clear as a bell. 'If that's another crank call, hang up!'

Shanti was watching me, her big brown eyes staring at me.

'He's not here. What's your name? I can take a message.'

'No. It's really important I speak to him . . . Can you give me a number where I can reach him?'

'He's out on police business, I'm afraid.'

The other policeman was still calling orders. 'Have they still not given you their name? Tell them if they don't tell you their name right now, you're hanging up!'

'Please! Don't hang up!' I yelled down the line.

PC Carey wanted to call out to his sergeant again, hand the phone and the responsibility over to him. He was a rookie, just weeks on the job. He had only arrived at the flat an hour ago to take over from the day shift. But his sergeant had just moved out of the room, leaving him in charge. 'Hang up!' had been his last order.

This caller was only a boy. Probably a hoax, a wind-up. The officers who had been here all day had told him the phone had been ringing constantly, and they had all been crank calls – oddballs coming out of the wood-work, claiming to know something about the so-called conspiracy theory.

JJ had a reputation for putting you through the wringer if you made mistakes. There had already been some incident he had to attend to. Apparently, he had

130

left the flat like a bat out of hell. Something pretty big. Who was this Jane Faulkner? This wasn't fair, PC Carey was thinking. He had been left at the crime scene and all he'd been told was that JJ wanted any calls that came in to be passed on to him. But surely he hadn't expected so many hoax calls? Surely he hadn't meant a call from a boy?

However, Carey thought it wiser not to risk any mistakes. 'Give me your number. I'll get him to call you back.'

The boy was talking fast. 'There's no time for that. It's really important I get in touch with him. I have to tell him about the conspiracy!'

Another conspiracy call! If he hadn't mentioned that, he might have believed the boy. That decided him. Teenage hoodlum, up to no good. He knew the type. 'Detective Inspector Julian is not here at the moment. The best I can do is take a message.'

He heard a girl's voice in the background. 'Tell him if he doesn't give you the number, he'll be in real trouble. You've got life-or-death information.'

He'd be in real trouble! Now he knew it was a wind-up.

'Look, son, you're the one who's going to be in real trouble,' he said as sternly as he was able. 'We haven't got time for your nonsense. This is a murder scene. Phone back later if it's so important.'

And he hung up.

37

I held the phone out to Shanti. 'Looks like I'm on my own again.' I flopped on to the sofa. I felt sick. 'That's what all the police will think – that I'm winding them up. I'm only a boy. No one's going to listen to me. What am I going to do?'

'You can't stop now.' Shanti heard the panic in my voice. 'You have to do something.'

Serena had been right. Now the door was opened, memories were trickling through ever faster. There was something I had to do here, somewhere I had to go. It was that somewhere that was the answer.

She was right about another thing. There was something I didn't want to remember. What could it be?

'He'll try to stop me,' I said. 'The Dark Man. I haven't seen the last of him.'

'You can't let him.' The voice came through from the bedroom, as quiet as the night. Serena's voice, weak but clear. 'Come here, Ram.'

Serena looked paler than ever, like alabaster. I drew in my breath. I suddenly realised why she looked familiar.

Sapphire Lennox, the missing girl, the ghost.

Serena saw my look, called me closer to her. 'You

looked at me that way earlier. What did you see?'

'Sorry, it's just that . . . Well, it was probably just my imagination, but last night –'

'He thinks he saw a ghost!' Shanti snapped. She glared at me, daring me to give her aunt any trouble.

'And I must look like a ghost already,' Serena said, smiling weakly. 'What happened?'

'I was in a graveyard. I saw a ghost. Sapphire Lennox's ghost.'

'Do you believe in ghosts?' Serena asked me.

'Of course I don't.'

'Then . . . what makes you think she was a ghost?'

'I don't know. She was dressed in white, she was scary . . . I don't know. What else could she be?'

And I realised as I said it how daft I sounded, and I asked myself that question: what else could she be? I didn't believe in ghosts. So what was the alternative?

Sapphire Lennox was missing. She'd been kidnapped.

Kidnapped by terrorists. They had to be holding her somewhere.

What if the figure I had seen had been real, alive – hadn't been a ghost at all? She had been trying to run away. She was distraught, her dress dirty. She was frightened.

I thought back to last night. I saw her again in my mind, saw her stumbling towards me, reaching out to me . . . not to frighten me at all, but reaching out for help. And I'd run from her.

But why would she be there, in a lonely graveyard, miles from anywhere?

Why had I been there?

A bit of a coincidence that I should stumble on the most famous missing person in Britain . . . and I no longer believed in coincidences.

It *was* no coincidence that I had been there.

I had been following the Dark Man, and he had led me there before I lost him. What had he been doing?

I heard his words to Salou again, clear in my mind: *We've put that somewhere appropriate. Somewhere no one will ever find it.*

And Salou's reply. *That should teach someone to keep their mouth shut.*

It was Sapphire Lennox they'd been talking about. Angus Lennox's 'little treasure'. It had to be.

She'd been kidnapped by the Dark Men to keep Angus Lennox quiet. To keep his mouth shut.

But why was she in the graveyard?

What do you do with treasure?

I sat on the bed. My mouth went dry. 'No . . .' I murmured in horror.

Because right then I knew exactly what they had done with her, where they had 'put' her. Somewhere 'appropriate'. A place no one would ever find her.

I remembered the open grave.

They'd buried her alive.

38

'They've buried her alive,' I said. I imagined that young girl enclosed in that dark, tight space, her air running out, terrified.

'They've given her father a deadline,' Serena said. She glanced at Shanti. 'Oh, I keep up with the news. Nothing much else to do when you're lying here.' She reached out and touched my hand – cold and bony, and yet comforting. 'Noon tomorrow, or she dies.'

'As long as her father keeps quiet they'll keep her alive.' I remembered him speaking directly into the cameras today on television. Had he been talking to the Dark Men, assuring them of his silence?

'Quiet about what?' Shanti said.

'I don't know – about the conspiracy, I guess. I heard the Dark Man and Salou talking about her – one of them called her their "little treasure". They wanted to teach someone a lesson in how to keep their mouth shut. It must be Lennox.' It made sense now. The pieces were falling into place. 'I think she must still be alive. If they'd just killed her, Angus Lennox would talk. But if he really believes there's a chance she's still alive . . .'

'You've figured all that out? You really must have

135

the gift.' Shanti tutted.

'Logic and observation, Shanti,' Serena said. 'Sometimes they are the greatest gifts we have.'

'What am I going to do?' I was almost talking to myself.

Shanti shook her head. 'I don't know. What can you do? You haven't got time to do anything for her. Not now. Anyway, if you can stop whatever it is that's going to happen tomorrow, you'll save her too.'

'Is that what you think, Ram? You haven't got time to save her?' Serena asked.

It wasn't what I thought at all. 'One person's life is as important as thousands. No one is expendable.' If I didn't keep believing that, I would believe nothing.

Expendable. A voice echoing the Dark Man and Ryan's dad, cold and scary. The voice of that other dark someone.

I knew I couldn't leave her there – a nightmare end to life. No. But who would believe me about this either? Shanti was right. How could I manage to do both? I had somewhere else to go, something else to do. Something was clearing in my head, like mist in the morning.

It came to me in a flash of inspiration. I looked at Shanti. 'You can save her. I'll tell you exactly where to find her, every detail.' Then hope was gone again. 'Except I don't know where this cemetery is. It can't be *that* far from Edinburgh . . . I got to the outskirts of the city after I ran. All I know is there was a deserted church, a gravestone. Owen Balfour's gravestone.' I saw it clearly in my head. '1892–1923. I'll never forget that.'

'If you saw all that, the police will be able to find

where it is in minutes,' Serena said.

'They will?'

'With computers, Ram. The internet. With that information, his name, the date of his birth and his death, they will find it.'

Shanti jumped to her feet. 'Just one thing, I'm not doing it. I can't leave you, Aunty. You need me.'

Serena managed to lean forward. 'You have to.'

Shanti's body stiffened. 'They'll want to know how I know all this.'

I had already thought about that. 'Tell them you have the gift. You've had visions of exactly where Sapphire Lennox is. You can lead them to her.'

She balled her hands into fists in anger. 'No way. It would be a lie. I don't have the gift.' I could see she hated having to admit that.

Serena assured her softly. 'You do have the gift, Shanti. It will come. You just don't know it yet.'

Shanti didn't want to do it. No doubt she'd have run from it if she could. But I saw then that she was going to, because her aunt had told her it was the right thing to do. 'I can't just leave you, Aunty. I don't want to.'

And I knew why. Her aunt was close to death. It might just come tonight. I could see that in Serena's eyes, in the transparent glow of her skin and the cold touch of her hand. There was a scent of death about the room.

But it wasn't a bad kind of scent. It was warm and comforting and filled the room like flowers. Death had come to lead Serena to a better place. I could almost picture him sitting in the corner, biding his time, like an old friend come to visit.

Did she imagine it too? Serena seemed to glance towards that same corner and smile. 'I'll be here when you come back, Shanti. I promise.'

'I'll never get away with it. They'll see through me right away and they'll laugh at me. I hate the thought of pretending I have the gift, having to convince them that I have special powers . . . and it's all him.' Shanti glared at me resentfully. 'I'm going to feel a fraud.'

'You're going to save someone's life, that's all that matters,' I told her. 'I have somewhere else I have to go.'

And the mist cleared – I knew where I was going and what I was going to do. I had been drawn there from the beginning – it was only now that I realised it.

'Hanover House. There are important people there,' I went on. 'Someone will believe me. Someone will listen. That's where I'm going.'

Shanti gasped. 'Do you know how tight the security is there? You don't honestly believe that you can just sneak into Hanover House?'

'No, Shanti. I'm going to be *caught* sneaking into Hanover House.'

39

'You're taking a big chance,' said Shanti.

'I have to,' I replied. 'It's the key. This conspiracy is something more than just bombing the peace marches. It's bigger than that. It's going to affect the whole country, maybe the entire world. That's why there are sleeper cells. I need to go where people can really do something about it. You said there were still important politicians and business leaders there. I'll get someone to listen.'

'But didn't you say this Dark Man worked for the government? What if he's there too?'

'I have to be prepared for that . . . but he can't do anything with all those important people around.' I only hoped that was true.

'I don't know why you need me, though.' Shanti was still reluctant to help. 'You can tell them about Sapphire Lennox too, can't you? They'll find her quicker than me.'

'Can't take the chance I don't get through to them in time. We can't let anyone die like that.'

'He's right, Shanti,' put in Serena. 'You have to do it.'

It was only because of her aunt she agreed. 'You

better tell me everything, then.'

So I told her quickly, tried not to leave out a single detail. I told her about the old deserted church and the gargoyles. About Owen Balfour's gravestone, the date of his death and the eerie inscription – *DEATH MAY SOON CALL YOU.*

'I tripped over the stone when I hauled myself out of the grave, so it has to be really close. And the gates – don't forget the gates. Snakes and skulls intertwined. They were so scary. They're locked. I had to climb over them. The grave must be newly dug fresh earth. The rest of the cemetery will be overgrown, so it should be easy to spot. It must be a few miles outside Edinburgh – in a secluded spot. I felt as if I was running for hours to get away from it. Do you really think they'll be able to find it?'

'They'll trace Owen Balfour by the date of his death. They'll find it,' Serena reassured me. 'Someone picked a good boy to save the world.' Her words made me flush with pride.

I took a deep breath. It was all about to happen. Going to Hanover House was the right thing. I could feel it, almost as if there was a voice inside my head, urging me to go there.

I looked at Serena and smiled. 'Thank you,' I said.

'And thank you, Ram. It was a pleasure meeting you.' She said it as if I would never see her again . . . I had a feeling she might be right.

'Thanks, Shanti, for helping me.' Would I ever see her again? I had only just met her and here I was, relying on her to save someone's life.

Yet I was sure I could trust her too.

'Good luck,' she said.

I took one last look at both of them, opened the door of the caravan and slipped out into the bustle of the fairground.

40

'How will I make them believe me?' Shanti said, watching as Ram zigzagged through the fair and disappeared among the crowds.

'They'll believe you, Shanti. You can make anyone believe anything. Now, you'd better go. Go quickly.'

Shanti pulled on her jacket. She went into the bedroom and kissed her aunt. 'Who am I, Aunty?'

She wanted to add that this might be her aunt's last chance to tell her. But how could she say such a thing?

'No time for that now. You'll know everything soon.' And her aunt lay back on her pillows and closed her eyes.

Shanti reluctantly left the caravan. There was no sign of Ram. He would be heading along the road towards the Hanover House estate. The crowds were growing; already people were screaming on the Waltzers and the Dodgems.

Was he really going to save the world from some terrible disaster? And was she actually going to save Sapphire Lennox from the worst death imaginable? It all seemed too big, unreal. She would wake up any moment and discover it had only been one of her dreams. How she wished she would.

She wished she'd never met him. Or that she'd let him jump from the back of the truck when she'd first seen him. She wished she was sitting in the caravan with her aunt, reading to her, looking forward to slipping from the caravan later, when her aunt was asleep, riding on the Big Wheel, watching the punters scream at the House of Fun, helping in one of those stalls – anything but this.

Pretending she had the gift. That was the worst thing.

She would feel a fraud.

Then she thought of Sapphire Lennox, deep in the ground, air running out, in the pitch-black. She thought of beetles and spiders and worms crawling over her, and she knew it didn't matter if they didn't believe she had the gift, that she was a charlatan, a fake. They would have to do something. And if she had to lie about having the gift, then so be it. She could never risk anyone dying like that.

Serena heard the door close quietly. Always such a thoughtful girl, Shanti. Serena was exhausted. Soon she would sleep. She wished she could have done more to help the boy. If Ben had been a different kind of man, she might have told Ram to go to him. But Ben would have dismissed his story as nonsense.

The boy was right. The police wouldn't believe him either.

She had seen things when the boy had spoken to her, things that even he hadn't seen. Things he was too afraid to remember. She should perhaps have told him, warned him. But no, he would have to find them out for himself. There were things he might never want to know. She had seen his past . . . and his future.

And Shanti? She so wanted to know the truth about herself. But how could Serena ever tell her? The truth was too dangerous. Ben would never allow it.

Shanti.

The gift would come to her. She was just the right age, the age when the gift had come to Serena herself. She might have to lie tonight, but soon her lies would be truth. And her lies would be worthwhile if they were to save someone's life.

She prayed Shanti would not be too late.

41

7.15 P.M.

The roads were busy as I left the fairground, plenty of people heading that way for a night of fun and enjoyment. No one took a second glance at me. Didn't they notice the determination on my face? Or the fear?

I followed Shanti's instructions and kept to the waterfront walkway that wound out of the town along the shore, running parallel with the train line to Glasgow. I was breathless by the time the walkway petered out across from the Hanover House estate. I could see the house, high up on the hill, its crow-stepped gables etched against the sky in the moonlight. I crossed the railway line and pushed my way through the trees, hardly taking my eyes from it.

Hanover House.

Surely there someone would listen to me, believe me. I would find an ally. I would find the truth at last.

Everything had been drawing me here since the beginning, I knew that now – drawing me to this house in Scotland. The people who would listen and do something about the conspiracy were all gathered here, working out a plan to defeat terrorism.

There was a line of protestors further up the road. I could hear them chanting, calling for peace, the brotherhood of man and an end to war. I could see their banners fluttering in the breeze.

The police presence was concentrated there. But Hanover House was part of a large estate. I hurried unseen across the road and leapt over a low wall that led to raspberry fields. I crouched and waited for alarms to go off, for floodlights to come on, exposing me, but nothing happened. No security in this part. The raspberry fields stretched up towards a wood. Beyond that was the house itself. It was there I guessed the real security would start.

I wanted them to catch me, but not too soon. I wanted to get as close to the house as possible, so they would take me there. I would demand it, tell them I had important information: that something was happening tomorrow and I didn't know what, but a dark conspiracy was behind it all.

Would I have done enough to stop it?

Stop it? Stop *what*? If only I could remember.

'*It's up to you.*'

The voice came again, clearer now, and it definitely wasn't mine. It sounded as if it was steps behind me. I swung round, half expecting to see him again, crouching behind the wall beside me.

The face of the Lone Bomber.

And then, it happened.

Like that feeling when you put your head underwater and all sounds fade. There was only silence. No traffic passing on the road, no distant sounds of the chanting crowds at the entrance to the estate. The world was on pause.

But how do I stop it? Help me.

It seemed as if everything around me faded into shadow. I was somewhere else, back in that underground tunnel.

'*It's up to you,*' the voice came again. And there he was, as solid as if he was right in front of me. I could see his face so clearly – his dark hair, his sad eyes. The Lone Bomber.

Why was he talking to me like this? Why were his eyes so sad? Was he crying?

I thought he was. I was sure I could see tears running down his face . . . and through the tears he was yelling at me, '*Get out of here! It's about to go off!*'

And I didn't want to go. I refused to go. I was yelling too, yelling and screaming.

He pleaded with me – '*Go! You have to go!*' – and pushed me away from him. It was so real to me that I could almost feel his hands on my shoulders, see his eyes so full of tears. So full of anger. And full of something else . . . something I couldn't understand.

And then, in a split second, like a lightning bolt, like a rocket zooming into the sky, I knew what that something was.

Love.

His eyes were filled with love for me.

And I knew then who he was, and it was like a spear going through my heart.

The lone bomber had been my father.

42

Shanti stepped into the police station at last. She had stood outside for ten minutes, not wanting to come in, not sure what to say when she did. She was nervous. She had never been so nervous. Her hands were sweating. She rubbed them down her jacket and did her best to stand tall and walk to the desk.

There was no one there. She looked around, finally noticing a bell and a card on the wall, which proclaimed: *Ring for Attention*.

She did just that, keeping her hand pressed against it so that it kept on ringing. Finally someone, an officer, came hurrying out of the back. He was wiping crumbs away from his mouth. Shanti wondered if it was his tea break. 'OK, OK, where's the fire?' he was saying.

He looked ancient, Shanti thought – too old to still be a policeman. He was almost bald and what hair he had was grey. But his eyes were clear and brown.

She had rehearsed what she was going to say all the way there, yet the words wouldn't come now. A lie. She was supposed to tell a lie, and she couldn't bring herself to do that.

'And what brings you here at this time of night? Are you lost?'

Her mouth was still too dry to answer him.

He looked behind her. 'Are you on your own? Where's your mum? Your dad?'

It was now or never. Shanti licked her lips and took a deep breath. 'I know where Sapphire Lennox is.'

I was shivering. Nothing to do with cold. Nothing to do with fear. The memories were making me shiver.

The Lone Bomber had been my father. Hadn't I known it, guessed it, feared it for so long?

I had almost seen it when Serena had probed my mind, but I had turned away too quickly, the memory too painful.

I didn't turn away now – couldn't even if I'd wanted to.

Memories of him began to tumble into my mind, like the acrobats at the fair. He'd been a soldier, and I had been so proud of him. I had loved watching him in his uniform – wanted so much to be like him. He had been the best kind of dad.

And then everything had changed.

There had been some kind of war, and he had come back a different man: nervous, always complaining, sure everyone was his enemy.

And I had grown to hate him.

He was certain they were out to get him, though he never could be sure who 'they' were. He had become paranoid. Yes, that was the word people had used to describe him, over and over. Paranoid. He saw conspiracies everywhere.

And he'd stopped being a soldier – I had hated that. They'd given him a job in the government, a desk job, and he couldn't handle that either. He was suspicious of everyone. Suspicious of people in high places, of politicians and civil servants – and finally they got fed up with his suspicions . . . and they had come to suspect *him*.

He was a perfect disciple to be recruited by the Dark Men, recruited into an even bigger conspiracy against the people he felt had betrayed him: the government, the country, the world.

So he had planted the bomb for them . . . and I had found out what he was going to do and had tried to stop him.

I put my hands over my ears to try to blot out the past. Serena had been right. I had seen his face when she had hypnotised me. That flicker of memory had been of my father. I had known deep down who he was, but when I saw his face I couldn't handle the truth.

I had tried to keep that door Serena had opened for me tight shut. I didn't want to remember this.

Was that another reason why I had run that day? The day of the explosion? I had tried to get as far away from him as possible, because I hated him for what he had done, what he'd become? That had to be the answer.

Had I put the memory of him so far to the back of my mind that I had pushed every other memory there too? The only explanation.

And what about my mother? Where was she? Why wasn't she looking for me? There was no record of me dying in the explosion, so why wasn't she searching for me?

I tried to remember a mother . . . and no picture came. She was still lost on the other side of that door.

And I had no time to think about it. Because maybe this was the way I could make up for what my father had done. Maybe that's what he had wanted me to do, why he had been calling to me, telling me it was up to me, I could stop it all. I hoped so. I was desperate to believe my father was good deep down, that he wanted out of the conspiracy – too late. I pulled myself to my feet.

I still didn't know everything.

But I knew enough.

43

8.10 P.M.

'Now why don't you just forget this nonsense and go home?'

'It is not nonsense. It's a matter of life and death.' Shanti was more sure of herself now. That big old policeman was trying to frighten her, and she would not be frightened. 'I'm not going to leave until you listen to me! Or would you prefer me to phone the BBC?'

'I'll tell you what,' the policeman said, moving closer. 'I'll take you back to the fair and we can see what your mum and dad think about this.'

She tried not to let that scare her. 'My mum . . . she's really ill. She knows I'm here. She would have come with me if she could. You're supposed to help people. I thought you would help me.'

She tried to sound like a little girl, vulnerable, frightened – the way she'd seen them do on TV programmes. It was even harder than lying.

Anyway, it wasn't working on this cop.

'I'll help you all right,' he said. 'Help you get home.'

Ram had been right. If he'd come here with his information, no one would have listened. Not in time anyway.

Well, she'd had enough. Shanti stood tall. Now was the time for some real acting. She began to scream at the top of her voice . . . and she wasn't going to stop until someone listened to her.

JJ called Emir Khan's flat. It was young PC Carey who answered the call.

'Forensics still there?'

'No, sir.'

'Any new developments?'

He seemed to hesitate before he answered. 'No, sir.'

'I'd like to know anything.' JJ had a feeling the lad was holding something back – probably nothing important, but JJ was an officer who liked to keep on top of every piece of information, no matter how trivial.

'We've had a lot of crank calls, sir.'

JJ was alert. 'What kind of crank calls?'

'Emir Khan put his number in the paper. They're all phoning up and saying they've got information. Most of them sound like they're from another planet.'

His joke didn't make JJ laugh.

'Did a boy call?'

'There was a caller who sounded young – had a girl with him. I heard her in the background. He was winding us up as well, sir.'

'Tell me exactly what he said.'

'Erm . . .' began the young PC, sounding nervous. 'He said he had to talk to you. He had some important information about "the conspiracy".'

JJ could visualise the inverted commas. 'He asked to speak to *me*, not Emir Khan . . . Is that what you're telling me, Carey?'

JJ could almost hear Carey cringing in the hesitation that followed, the penny dropping. 'Yes, sir, he asked to speak to you.'

'Why didn't you inform me of this right away?'

Carey's voice croaked. 'I thought it was just another crank call, sir. Sorry, sir.'

JJ couldn't blame young Carey. He had hoped the boy would call back. He should have been prepared for that. He would not make that mistake again.

'Right,' he said. 'This is what we're going to do.'

How long did I stay behind the wall? Didn't know. It took all my strength to move, because I didn't want to move, didn't want this responsibility.

But I had no choice. I began to crawl, making my way through the raspberry canes, heading for the wood that surrounded the house, watching constantly, listening, waiting for the moment when I would be spotted. Once I got through the wood, it wouldn't be long before the CCTV cameras would pick me up. No doubt about that. I was banking on it.

There was a little brook running through the wood. Just as I reached it, I heard dogs barking wildly in the distance, coming closer. I only prayed they were on a lead. I darted away from the sound, splashed into the water and crossed to the other side. I could make out movements through the trees, and men's voices now, calling to each other, coming for me.

I wanted to get as close to the house as I could, kept running, pushing my way through the trees, leaping over bushes. I knew I could never outrun those dogs. How many of them there were I didn't know, but they were not just behind me now. The barking seemed to be all around me – to the left, the right, howling towards me. I tripped and fell but was up in an instant. Some instinct to get away from those dogs was deep within me. I could hardly breathe with the fear of them. They were too close.

It was the barbed wire that stopped me at last – a fence of it running along the edge of the line of trees. I didn't see it, ran right into it, and when I attempted to climb over, my clothes became entangled. I tried to pull myself free. The wire tore at my hands. I was wrapped in it, couldn't move. The dogs were baying and barking ever closer. I turned my head and it was like some nightmare vision leaping towards me: Dobermanns, at least six of them, from all directions, jaws open, their teeth white against their dark faces.

44

The dogs jumped at me. They were all over me. They didn't have to hold me down – I was trapped in barbed wire. Their jaws dripped saliva on to my face. I was terrified.

'Down!'

It was the man's voice that stopped them tearing me apart, I was sure of it. I didn't even see him come up behind them. He looked puzzled when he saw me.

'Do you know where you are?' the man snarled at me. He was dressed from head to toe in black, wearing a protective vest, carrying a gun. In the dark it was hard to make him out at all.

I swallowed. 'Hanover House.' My voice sounded shaky. I was still under a vicious blanket of Dobermanns. 'Get these off me, will you?'

He took a moment to think about that. 'Back!' One word and the dogs moved away from me. 'Now get to your feet.'

I tried. I winced with pain as my hand tore on the wire. My sleeve was still caught. He didn't move to help me. Did he think I was going to suddenly attack him?

'I'm only a boy,' I said.

'Boys have been known to be suicide bombers,' was his answer. He searched me quickly. Then he spoke into a mike on his vest. 'It's a boy. Unarmed. I've got him.'

'I need to talk to someone,' I said. 'At the house. I have important information.'

His face settled into a smile. 'You?'

I took a step forward. He pointed the gun towards me.

'Yes, me. Now who's in charge here? I have to talk to them. I really do have important information.'

He seemed to think about that. 'You're going inside, don't worry about that.'

He grabbed me roughly by the shoulder, gripping not only my jacket, but my skin as well. I tried to struggle free but he held me fast. The Dobermanns danced beside him, jaws slavering, eyes never leaving me. They looked as if they'd eat me first chance they got.

We broke through the trees and, all at once, Hanover House was there in front of me. As I gazed up at it, the wind caught the bare branches of the trees and they moved like bony fingers scratching the clouds. There were lights on in several of the large windows on the ground floor and on the floors above. On the lawns around the house a line of trees, most of them winter bare, stretched into the distance. The small brook that surrounded the house curved between them into deep woods.

An idyllic setting.

It took my breath away – because I suddenly realised I knew this place. I could picture inside the ornate front door to the carved banister that led to the upper storeys.

I could see the polished wooden floors, the stained-glass windows.

I had been here before. That thought alone made me jerk to a halt. I was dragged on. No time to try to remember when I was here . . . or why.

But I had been inside Hanover House before.

45

The woman police officer was shaking Shanti, trying to get her to stop screaming. It had finally worked. They had brought someone else – someone young, someone female. Surely she would listen?

'Get a hold of yourself, girl!' The young woman's voice was abrupt, her face grim. Shanti began to wonder if she *would* listen.

She was finding it hard to stop shaking. Screaming, she decided, took a lot out of you. She took a deep breath. 'He won't believe me.' Her eyes moved to the big policeman. He looked thoroughly fed up with her. He rolled his eyes.

Shanti went on quickly. 'I know it's hard to believe. It's even hard for me to believe, but I'm not making it up. I know where Sapphire Lennox is. She's not dead. Not yet. But she will be if we don't hurry. I can tell you exactly where she is.

'She saw it in the stars,' the policeman said sarcastically.

'I did not!' Shanti snapped. She clutched at the

159

policewoman's hand. It was now she would have to lie. She braced herself, tried not to feel too much of a fake.

'I can feel it. I can't explain why.' And that at least was the truth. 'I've had these . . . visions. I keep seeing her, seeing where she is. It's as if she's leading me there. I didn't understand it myself at first, didn't believe it. I thought it was only dreams I was having . . . but the gift runs in the family.'

Her voice broke at that point. *No, it doesn't*, she was thinking. *I haven't got the gift, and never will . . . because I'm not one of the family*.

'Go on,' the policewoman urged her.

'I can save her. You have to believe me.'

'We've had lots of crank calls about this. People saying they have information about Sapphire Lennox. There's a big reward. Why should we believe you?'

'I don't want any reward.' She would refuse to take it – hadn't known anything about that anyway. 'You can't afford to ignore me.' Shanti's voice was suddenly sure and confident. 'Because she's been buried alive, and she's running out of air.'

I was dragged round the back of the house. The security guard held on to me while he tied up the Dobermanns. In fact, he was almost holding me up. I was in shock. So many things were coming back to me at once.

I knew what I was going to see inside here – had seen it before. The large conservatory with the long conference table, the high-backed chairs placed around it. My mind was trying to grapple with all of this. When had I been here . . . and why?

We went through the conservatory and into a grand sitting room. Two red leather chesterfield sofas were ranged on either side of a tall ornate fireplace. A roaring fire burned in the grate. Walnut bookcases lined the walls.

I remembered this room too; I was certain I had seen the desk in the corner before, the computer, the green lamp, the telephone. I knew, without thinking about it, that the walls in this room opened up and led to deep closets, and even a cocktail cabinet. I felt myself start to sway.

'Are you going to faint?' the man asked me.

I almost was, memories leaping at me because I was in this room. I'd been afraid here . . . Why?

The man in black pushed me into one of the leather chairs. 'You sit and don't move till I can get someone.' He pointed to the cameras on the wall. 'And don't forget, you're being watched all the time.'

I couldn't speak. I was trembling. He walked back through the conservatory and I was left alone.

Or not. The cameras focused on me. I could imagine people in another room, watching my every move.

Let them watch. I wasn't doing anything wrong. I was here to warn them of a conspiracy. There were important people here who would help. Wasn't that why I'd come?

What was I going to tell them? *Something big is going to happen tomorrow. You have to stop it.*

And by the way, my father was the Lone Bomber.

No. I could never tell anyone that, never come out of

the shadows now. I'd warn them and then I would slip away. I was the son of the Lone Bomber. I could think of nothing worse.

Even now, sitting by that roaring fire, I could see his face so plainly. It had been his voice I had heard so often in my nightmares.

Yet it seemed in those final moments he had only wanted to save me, to stop what was happening. That should have made me forgive him, but it didn't. He could have killed thousands with that bomb. Thousands of innocent people.

I could never forgive that.

I watched the door, waiting for someone to come through, ready for anything.

'Time's running out! It's up to you.'

It had been my father who had shouted that at me. *'Get out of here . . . stay safe. Only you can stop it.'*

Flashing images flickered in my mind. Things were coming back to me so fast I felt light-headed. The underground car park, damp and cold. My dad pushing me away, telling me to run. Telling me to . . . *stop it*.

Too many things burst into my mind at once. I couldn't take them all in. My dad always warning people about conspiracies, nobody listening.

Conspiracies.

He'd been right all along. This was the biggest conspiracy in history, threatening the whole world. He'd been part of it . . . hadn't he? So why was he telling me to stop it? Why the sudden change of heart?

Every time I thought I knew the whole truth, another truth surfaced.

Black spots in front of my eyes. I thought for a moment I would faint.

Because suddenly, I was sure at last I knew it all.

I had followed my dad, run down into that car park . . . so certain my father had been planting the bomb . . . and I was going to stop him making the biggest mistake of his life . . .

But he hadn't been planting the bomb.

He'd been trying to defuse it.

46

'You'd better be telling the truth, young lady.' How often did they have to say that to her? Their faces were sceptical. They had insisted on phoning her aunt, and when Shanti had begged them not to, it had only made them more suspicious. Aunt Serena's voice had been weak but firm. 'She's telling the truth. She was afraid you wouldn't believe her. But please, she is telling the truth.'

Shanti had been angry when they'd called her aunt, but at least it had made them begin to think she might not be making all this up. Shanti had stared them down. 'There's no time to waste. So you'd better believe me.' She could repeat things too.

At last they had someone on the line who was in charge of the investigation. The WPC – 'call me Dorothy,' she had said – held the phone out to her. 'Tell him everything.'

Shanti's hand was shaking as she took the phone. She drew in a deep breath. This was all going to sound so unbelievable. 'Sapphire Lennox has been buried alive. They've left her with enough air, but it's going to run out soon. I don't think they have any intention of saving her.'

Why had she said that?

'And I hear you saw this in a vision?'

There it was again, that scepticism.

'What does it matter?' She tried not to shout, but it was hard. She didn't want them to ask that question. No. She didn't want to have to answer it. She didn't want to lie.

'I can tell you exactly where to go.'

There was a long pause on the line. She could picture them all, the detectives on the case, looking round at each other, shaking their heads, believing nothing she had to say.

'OK,' the senior policeman said at last. 'Where do we find her?'

Shanti closed her eyes. She concentrated and tried to repeat to them all that Ram had told her. It had been an isolated, ruined church, he had said – had to be somewhere near Edinburgh. Gravestones were clustered around it. It was isolated, no light from any nearby town. Broken gravestones, unkempt, uncared for . . . apart from one newly dug grave. Shanti's bones quivered at the thought of what that grave now held. She told them of the padlocked iron gates entwined with snakes and skulls. And the name on the gravestone, its inscription:

OWEN BALFOUR
1899–1923
DEATH MAY SOON CALL YOU

She remembered it all, and it was so vivid in her mind she almost felt she *had* been there herself.

'How can you describe it so clearly?' The policeman's

165

voice was suspicious, the faces all around her suspicious.

'How does she know all this?' said another sceptical voice on the line, somewhere in the background.

She was fed up with their attitude. She snapped back. 'Because that's how visions work. You wouldn't know because you don't have the gift!'

She didn't have the gift either, but there was no way she was admitting to that now. She knew she sounded sure of herself. She had almost convinced herself, she had such a vivid picture of it in her head.

The policeman in charge was convinced too.

'Stay by the phone. We're going to trace that grave-yard.'

47

8.30 P.M.

It was as if a dam had burst in my brain.

My dad had known about the bomb, had known about the whole conspiracy.

I had thought he was one of them, one of the Dark Men. I had found out where he was going that day, sure I knew about the terrible thing he was planning to do. And all the time he had been going there to defuse it. He had tried to stop the bomb going off.

He'd been too late.

No wonder I had lost my memory.

Yet he had saved my life, saved all those people's lives. No one had died. No one except my dad. He had saved me. He had pushed me away and he had to run in there, back down into that underground car park, and the last thing he had said to me was, 'Only you can stop it.'

I wasn't asking any more what it was I had to stop, because now I remembered. And it had nothing to do with the peace marches.

Everything clicked into place. I had even seen it all before, imagined it happening today, in the station.

I'd seen the world in flames, everywhere, all at the same time.

Worst-case scenario. Everything happening at once, causing confusion, panic, chaos. The world was already on high alert for something. But this?

The President of the United States – assassinated, tomorrow. Air Force One blown up in mid-air. The trigger for everything else.

And all those other leaders – killed, blown up, shot, assassinated, dying on their way back to their home countries.

Bombs going off, landmarks destroyed, suicide planes being flown into cities all over the world. A worldwide coordinated attack killing thousands, millions maybe, bringing down governments. Emergency services unable to cope, governments unable to cope. International panic. People desperate for order to be restored.

And the Dark Men of the world stepping in and taking over.

And it was all going to happen tomorrow.

And then I remembered what it was called – knew at last where my name came from.

Operation Ram.

48

It seemed like an age before anything happened. Shanti sat at the desk. No one spoke to her. No one spoke at all. What was happening? No one was telling her anything. They were trying to trace the graveyard. Surely it shouldn't take them that long, not with the internet.

She jumped when the phone rang. Dorothy answered – it only took a few seconds.

'Right, they know where the graveyard is. They're on their way there now. We've got to get in the car – meet them there. Come on, get your coat.'

Shanti hadn't expected this. 'I don't want to go. I have to get back to my aunt.'

They didn't need her now, surely?

'I'll call your aunt, Shanti,' Dorothy said. 'You can talk to her, but I'm sure she won't object.'

Shanti felt sick. She knew her aunt would agree to her going. But it was one thing telling them what Ram had told her . . . quite another to actually go to the place herself.

Dorothy was a real misery. Her face didn't crack into a smile once. As she led Shanti to the waiting car, she was eyeing her suspiciously.

Maybe, Shanti thought, *they're thinking I have something to do with the kidnapping since I know so much.*

What had she got herself into?

No time to think any more. The door opened; I stood up. A man came in, heavy set, bushy eyebrows. I knew his face from somewhere.

He was a politician. Chancellor of the Exchequer? Deputy Prime Minister. Wasn't sure. It didn't matter. He was the man in charge.

'I have something really important to tell you. Something's going to happen tomorrow. A massive terrorist attack. Air Force One is going to be blown up somewhere over the Atlantic. That will be the trigger for the whole thing. You have to stop it. It's called Operation Ram.'

He looked at me in disbelief. I couldn't blame him for that. 'It's true.' I went on. 'It's all going to start tomorrow. All over the world. Bombs exploding, water supplies infected, bridges blown up.' Every second, more was coming back to me.

'Why would anyone do such a thing?'

'To take power. There will be chaos everywhere – people will want someone to bring order back . . . and the Dark Men will step in across the world.'

A chill went through me as I remembered. They were all in high-powered positions . . . but not quite the top spots . . . not yet. Not until tomorrow.

'So you've remembered.'

'Yes. It's all coming . . . back.' I stepped away from

him. 'H-how did you know I'd lost my memory?'

He didn't need to answer that one. How stupid had I been? If I'd had another few seconds I would have remembered the whole thing. The Dark Men were already in place, here at Hanover House. They'd convened from all over the world, waiting to take over when the time came. The leaders of the countries had left the conference already . . . and they would be dealt with. The ones remaining . . . they were the Dark Men, safe until it was all over, making their plans, waiting.

When tomorrow came, the world would want them to take over, plead with them to restore order – in any way they wanted.

Too late. I had remembered . . . moments too late.

There were too much to remember all at once, too much for a boy to take in. It wasn't fair. I had a feeling like I'd never had before, as if the earth was turning under my feet, as if I was balancing on a rubber ball. I closed my eyes. I had walked right into the spider's web. Hanover House.

Why had my dad ever trusted me? I had done all the wrong things. The one thing I shouldn't have done was come here. Now I was trapped. I could stop nothing. The man with the bushy eyebrows stepped back. Another figure entered the room.

It was the Dark Man.

49

8.40 P.M.

The Dark Man was smiling.

'Deal with him,' the other man said coldly. And he left.

'We really will have to stop meeting like this,' he said, at his most charming – and his most dangerous.

He wasn't alone. Another man came in behind him – older, in a grey suit. Could have been someone's favourite uncle.

How was I going to escape? What was the point?

'*Never give up, Ram.*'

I was sure it was my dad's voice I heard. It gave me courage.

I had to stay alert. I pressed the wounds on my hands. The pain pulled me back to the present – away from all those memories. I would escape, or be killed trying. I glanced behind me. Could I make it out of the conservatory? The vicious barks of the Dobermanns gave me my answer. Too close, too close. But there had to be some escape.

'I'm not going to hurt you.'

172

'Right, like I'm going to believe that.' My eyes were going from his to the other man. He was moving closer too. I was afraid of what they had in mind.

'Now you're here, you can do nothing to stop us. There's no point in hurting you, can't you see?'

'Just let me go, I won't say anything. I promise.'

And this time it was the Dark Man's turn to say, 'Like I'm going to believe that.'

They were on either side of me now, the other man edging closer.

'This is the doctor,' the Dark Man said.

And I looked and saw now that the other man was holding something in his hand. A syringe.

'Just let him give you one little injection, and –'

'And I'm dead. No way.'

The Dark Man shook his head. 'I've never wanted you dead. You should know that. I could have killed you many times. I just didn't want you to remember.'

They couldn't afford for me to remember, he had told me in a lift shaft only a few weeks ago.

The doctor was dangerously close. I moved back, my eyes never leaving that syringe.

'Well, I do. I remember everything. I remember my dad . . . I remember he saved me. So what are you going to do about it?'

'Let the doctor do his work and you'll have a different kind of memory when you wake up.'

I didn't understand at first. A different kind of memory? Then I realised what he meant and it was scarier than anything else. Scarier than torture, than death. They were going to plant a false memory in me. It was bad enough having no memory, but having one that wasn't mine at all? No way. It didn't bear thinking about.

'When you wake up you'll realise how pointless all this is. You've been running all this time for nothing.' His eyes were violet, turning to black. The most menacing shade I had ever seen. I had called him Mr Death once . . . and that's what he seemed to be again. Mr Death.

'Give in,' he said. 'Can't you see that I've won?'

50

Detective Inspector Graham, the officer in charge of the Lennox investigation, was supposed to be going off duty until this happened. Why on earth were they believing the word of some daft wee lassie? He'd had hardly any time off since the girl was kidnapped, and his wife was making him his favourite dinner tonight – steak and kidney pie – and instead of getting stuck into that, here he was racing in a police car to some graveyard in the middle of nowhere.

'How far is this place?' he asked at last.

The driver glanced in his mirror. 'It's not far now, sir,' he said, in a tone that indicated he wished he was somewhere else too.

'Time's running out!' the detective said sarcastically. 'I can't believe we're listening to a kid. She's got to be making all this up – just wants her fifteen minutes of fame.' He let out a long sigh. 'Oh well, this wasn't the kind of lead I was hoping for . . . but it's the only one we've got.'

175

I'd never let him win. I couldn't.

I bolted for the conservatory, even though I could hear more dogs out there, barking madly, blocking any escape that way. At the last second I leapt towards the window. The Dark Man was right behind me. I threw the heavy curtains at him, ducked behind them, was lost in them. He grabbed me and pulled me free of them. I filled the room with my fists and my feet, kicking out at him, punching at him, moving all the time for the door, never giving him a minute. He could get no hold of me at all.

But the doctor was at the door now, standing against it, that syringe held like a dagger in front of him.

There was no way out. I felt the Dark Man grab at my arm. I pulled it free, scrabbled over the desk to get away from him. I would run for the conservatory again, risk the Dobermanns, try to push past the men outside – the men waiting with guns. I couldn't let them get me now. Not now that I had remembered everything.

No false memory for me.

It was my hair he grabbed this time, pulling it by the roots. I let out a yelp. Then his fingers closed round my neck, hauling my head back so far I had to look up at him. I had to keep my head.

Don't panic, Ram.

The doctor was advancing towards me and no matter how I kicked and struggled I was held fast by the Dark Man.

It couldn't end this way. After everything I had been through it couldn't just end with a simple injection, making me forget the truth. Making me only remember a lie.

'Now, just relax,' the doctor said, as if he was some kindly GP come on a visit. 'This isn't going to hurt.'

51

'Don't suppose you remember the road from that vision of yours?' Drippy Dorothy glared at Shanti in the mirror.

Was she supposed to remember seeing all of this? What *did* you see if you had the gift? Was it an actual vision? Was it sounds, or just feelings? Shanti felt as if she was falling into a black hole, one lie leading to another. She should have asked her aunt to tell her exactly what she should say, so she didn't make any glaring mistakes. Soon they would reach this cemetery, and she would be as lost as they were. She'd never be able to keep up the pretence. They'd put her in jail for sure. How did she ever get herself into all of this?

Dorothy was still scowling at her, and that was really getting up Shanti's nose. She at least had to act confident, as if she knew what she was talking about. 'You'll be there soon,' Shanti said with authority. 'Not far now.'

It was desperation that gave me courage. I went limp, as if I had given up, as if I was ready to slip into unconsciousness even without the drug. I fell against the Dark Man, and his grip on me loosened ever so slightly – all I needed. I threw up my legs and made a furious lunge at the doctor. I caught them both by surprise. The doctor staggered back. I was out of the Dark Man's grip. As the doctor stumbled, I grabbed the syringe, turned it and stabbed at him. He crumpled. His eyes went wide. The needle stuck out of his neck. He tried to pluck it free of him – I didn't give him a chance. I swung him round so he fell against the Dark Man, giving me seconds more, just seconds, to run for the door of the room.

I hauled it open, ready to dodge anyone who was there. But there was no one. They obviously thought I was being taken care of – no threat. Think again!

I made for the front door, but at the last moment I could see through the frosted glass that someone was standing there, and knew by the sound of barking that there was a Dobermann with him. No escape there.

I swivelled round. The Dark Man was right behind me. I dodged round a table in the centre of the hallway, pushed a massive vase of roses towards him. He tried to catch it and missed. The vase fell against him, water and flowers went everywhere.

He shouted, 'Stop that boy!'

Where did they all suddenly come from? People emerged from rooms and passages, some with guns. I leapt for the staircase, began to run.

A shot rang out – so loud it almost burst my eardrums, and a bullet exploded into a wall nearby. Still I ran. At the top of the stairs a man appeared, another face I vaguely recognised. He looked surprised to see me. I rammed into him, head down, sent him sprawling. But I held on to him, turned him and pushed. He went rolling down the staircase, yelling, sending others tumbling as they tried to climb the stairs.

I ran along the corridor. Someone else was heading for me. I took another set of stairs, three at a time.

How would I get out of this one? I didn't even know where I was going. I had to do something, warn somebody. They had to know about this place, about what was happening at Hanover House. About the plot. But how could I do it now? Who could I trust?

JJ.

Even as I ran, that strong dependable voice came back to me. JJ. If only I had managed to get through to him.

There was nowhere else to run. I came to the last room in the corridor and skidded in. It was some kind of office – desks, phones and computers. I pushed the door closed and turned the key in the lock. By the wall there was a table. It looked so heavy I doubted at first I could push it to bar the door. But slowly, I did.

It would only give me minutes more, then they would be here, they would burst through. I looked around but there were no other doors in the room. There was no other way out. Only the window.

Could I jump? But I was three floors up. It was a long way down, and already I could hear those hounds of hell outside, baying for my blood.

At any moment they would come pounding at the door. I backed up against the desk and prayed.

I needed a miracle.

52

When they pulled up at the gates there were already another two police cars waiting. Dorothy stepped from the car and stood for a moment, looking at the gates. Then she turned to Shanti.

'You described them perfectly.'

And she had. Shanti couldn't have described them better if she had seen them herself. Snakes entwined round the spikes, serpents' heads spewing out of the open mouths of skulls. What twisted mind had thought this up? It made her feel sick.

Four uniformed policemen stepped from one of the cars, and from the other a medic and a man in a dark suit. It took Shanti only a moment to recognise him. Angus Lennox. He strode across to her, his face stern.

'You must be the girl who says she knows where my daughter is.'

Shanti said nothing, not sure what she could say – tell him now about Ram?

One of the other policeman called to him. 'If she's right, we've no time to waste, sir,' he said.

Lennox nodded and turned from her.

Shanti saw then that they were all carrying spades.

The gates were closed. Heavy iron chains were wound through the bars and padlocked. 'We'll have to climb over,' someone said.

The night was chill and quiet. A perfect night for a little grave robbing, Shanti thought.

'I'm coming too,' she said.

Dorothy held her back, but Detective Inspector Graham looked over and nodded. 'Let her come,' he said.

Shanti grabbed the railings and hauled herself up. She was the first one over. There was an urgency now in the police officers' movements. Shanti could sense what they were thinking. She'd been right about the grave-yard, right about the gates. What else was she right about?

53

9.05 P.M.

The Dark Man pounded at the door. It was locked and barred from the inside – a solid door, not like the ones in movies that could be barged through with a shoulder.

'He can't get away,' the man beside him said. 'There's no escape.'

But he knew the boy, knew that he'd find a way if there was one. 'Get someone at the window in case he jumps,' he whispered back. 'I know another way to get in this room.'

He ran back along the corridor and into the next room. From there, he knew there was a connecting door. It was disguised as a bookcase in this room, and looked like an ordinary oak wall panel in the room the boy was in. There was no way he could know that there was a secret door. And he wasn't likely to leap from the window, not from the third floor. There were no other exits. The boy was trapped.

The Dark Man entered the bookcase silently, pushed the panelled wall open and stepped into the room.

The boy was there, at the desk. He turned quickly

when he heard the door opening. His face was chalk white. He was shaking.

'There's no escape,' the Dark Man said. 'Give it up. You've done your best but it's too late. I told you before you can't win. It's all going to begin tomorrow, and you can't stop it.'

The boy was breathless, but his voice cool and clear. 'I've remembered everything now . . . A coordinated worldwide attack, starting tomorrow. Operation Ram.'

'I knew as soon as I heard you were calling yourself by that name that it would come back to you. I knew when you first turned up here in Scotland that you would remember eventually.'

'I came to Hanover House thinking someone would help me. I thought all these top people were the good guys, but they're not, are they?'

'Hanover House is our base of operations – always has been.'

'And all the people left here, the politicians, everybody . . . part of the conspiracy? Part of Operation Ram?'

What was the point of not telling him? the Dark Man thought. The boy deserved the truth. 'Every single one. We're ready to take over when the world falls apart.'

'And it's going to start tomorrow, with Air Force One blowing up over the Atlantic,' the boy said.

'That's right. The most powerful man in the world goes and, like dominoes, all those other world leaders die after him.'

The boy was shaking his head as if he couldn't take it in. 'But America has a Vice President. He'll take over. You won't have changed a thing.'

'The Vice President is one of us.'

The boy drew in his breath. He hadn't remembered that, it seemed.

'We have people in place across the world, ready to take over when the panic begins,' the Dark Man continued. 'And it will, and we'll keep the panic mounting with more bombings, more assassinations, with water supplies being polluted – can't you see what a great plan it is? The world is sick of terrorism; it needs people to deal with it. And we are the people to do that.'

'Wait a minute . . . you're *causing* all the terrorism.'

'Yes, this time . . . but the terrorist cells we have working for us are under our control. They're part of the operation. The end justifies the means, as they say.'

He stepped forward. The boy backed against the desk, afraid. 'Can't you see the brilliance in this plan? We're going to take over the world . . . and the world is going to be grateful.'

'But why? What's wrong with the world as it is?'

'This world won't survive and prosper unless it has strong leadership; leadership willing to make hard decisions. After tomorrow, we'll stamp out terrorism and no one will question our methods. No one will stand against us.'

'But why? I still don't understand.'

'Do you realise that by 2020 the climate, the population of the world, they'll be out of control. There won't be enough food, enough water, unless someone does something about it – *now*. We will. We'll take the tough decisions. And if that means trimming the herd, then that's what we'll have to do.'

185

'Trimming the herd?' That puzzled the boy.

'Survival of the fittest. It's how mankind has always grown. If we don't do something now, mankind's not going to survive this century. We're going to make the world a better place.' He smiled. 'It's a kind of tough love. You've heard of that, right?'

'That's what you meant by saying people are expendable. And you'll decide who is and who isn't?'

'Yes. We'll decide.'

'You're mad . . .' The boy's eyes glazed over, thinking it through. 'And it all began with the bombing in London . . .'

'Then one bomb after another to heighten the paranoia about terrorism, to make people believe and be afraid that there are terrorists round every corner.'

'But the so-called Lone Bomber wasn't part of your conspiracy, was he? He was never part of the conspiracy. Tell me!' There was desperation in the boy's voice.

The Dark Man knew how vital it was for the boy to know that, and he didn't mind telling him – not now. 'Of course he wasn't.'

'He didn't plant the bomb that day, did he?'

'No, he –'

'He was a hero, not a villain, not like you. He wasn't planting the bomb.' The boy was suddenly shouting. 'He was defusing it, wasn't he? *Wasn't he?*'

'Yes! You're right. He was defusing the bomb. He was never part of the conspiracy. Are you happy now?'

For a moment, he thought the boy was going to cry – he lowered his head. But when he raised it again and looked directly at him, it seemed a dark smile had spread across his face.

The Dark Man was puzzled. The boy slowly stepped to the side of the desk . . . and there was the phone, lying on its side.

The boy shouted into it. 'Did you get that, JJ? Did you hear it?'

And a man's voice called out loud and clear. 'Every word. Had it on loudspeaker – taped and copied. Operation Ram. We're alerting our international security networks right now . . . and we're on our way to Hanover House.'

The boy stood tall, and yelled, 'You told them everything! You! Not me. You did. I win!'

54

I had never seen a man so angry. His face flushed red, his dark eyes flashed. He tried to snatch the phone from me, but he was too late.

'You might as well give up now.' I threw his own words back at him.

But I knew by the anger in his eyes he would never give up. Well, neither would I.

He leapt at me and I lifted the receiver lying on the desk and smashed it against his face. I had the satisfaction of seeing blood spurt from his nose.

My heart was pumping. He covered his face with his hands, and I took the opportunity to dodge past him. I was out of the door he had come through. No one waited there. They must have thought the Dark Man was dealing with me.

And I had fooled him. I'd had one last chance as they pounded on the door. Remembering how clearly I had heard the other man's voice when I'd phoned Emir Khan's number to speak to JJ, I'd grabbed the phone and dialled Emir Khan's number again. Someone had to be there. Someone who would listen. Someone who would help me.

And my one piece of luck.

JJ had had all Emir's calls transferred straight to his mobile.

My miracle.

But I had no time to tell JJ everything. I knew the Dark Man would find a way in. It was JJ who had told me to stay on the line, to hide the phone, get the Dark Man to talk – and he would hear it all.

And the Dark Man had told them everything.

He would come after me. He would never let go. And this time I didn't think he would hesitate to kill me.

The police were coming to Hanover House. They knew about Operation Ram.

I had stopped it . . . 'Dad,' I said silently, 'we did it.'

With the help of the Dark Man.

I glanced behind me. There was no sign of him. Where was he? Then I realised – he must be warning the others. Warning them to get out.

I couldn't let that happen. JJ was coming with support . . . but maybe not fast enough.

How could I get help here sooner?

I leant against the wall and tried to think. Already doors were banging. I could hear shouts and cries. Things were beginning to move.

What else could I do? How could I bring more police to Hanover House?

And there, right in front of me, the answer.

The fire alarm.

If it went off, it would alert the fire stations in the surrounding towns. They would race here, especially because this was Hanover House. There were important people here. They didn't know how important. The police would come too, simply because this was Hanover House. They wouldn't take any chances.

IN CASE OF EMERGENCY SMASH GLASS

You don't get more of an emergency than this, I thought. I looked around for something to smash the glass with. There was a bronze statue on a table against the wall, some kind of angel, her arms held above her. That was exactly what I needed. An angel. I lifted it, smiled at the weight of it. Then I swung it as hard as I could against the glass box.

55

The lights from the police torches beamed along the ground. They had spread out to look for Owen Balfour's gravestone, but it was nowhere to be found.

'The place has been vandalised,' Dorothy said to Shanti. 'If there was an Owen Balfour here, his stone's broken up now. Impossible to read.' She bent down, shone her torch on one of the only stones still left intact. Not Owen Balfour's.

'And there are no new graves,' one of the other officers said. He was right. Everything was overgrown, as if the ground hadn't been disturbed in centuries. 'I knew this was a blinking wild goose chase.'

'You must be wrong, Shanti,' Dorothy said.

Angus Lennox turned to Shanti and spoke to her directly. 'Do you still believe my daughter is somewhere here?'

She looked into his eyes – eyes filled with grief and worry. 'You know who took her, don't you?' she asked him softly.

He started, a look of guilty panic flashing across his face.

'I do.' His voice was barely a whisper.

'When we find her, will you tell the police

191

everything you know?'

'Alive or dead, if they've done this awful thing to her . . . I'll tell them everything. But I've got to find her first.'

Shanti closed her eyes. She tried to block out their voices, tried to remember exactly what Ram had told her. Sapphire Lennox had to be here, somewhere under this hard ground. He'd been right about the church and the gates. There had to be something else, something she'd forgotten. She could hear her aunt's voice whispering, 'Logic and observation, Shanti – sometimes that's all you need.'

Owen Balfour's stone had only been recently vandalised. She would stake her life on that. They had done it, the people who had kidnapped Sapphire. Shanti could almost see them do it, breaking up a recognisable landmark so that, if and when the time came, no one would be able to find her. Logic.

Shanti was breathing hard, taking in great gulps of air.

Dorothy touched her arm. 'Are you OK?' she asked, concerned.

Shanti shook her head. She knew why her breathing was becoming so difficult. She was imagining Sapphire running out of air.

'Should we start digging?' she heard one of the policeman ask.

She had to be able to give them more information, otherwise they could be digging for hours. And Sapphire didn't have hours.

She was picturing Ram again, stumbling through the dark cemetery, afraid. Her eyes snapped open. She looked at the church carved into the skyline, watched the flickering of the torches as their beams panned the ground.

One of them caught something.

'What's that!' she called.

The policeman trained the light back.

'There!' she yelled.

Something was fluttering on the branches of a rowan tree. A piece of material. Green material. She was sure she recognised it, had seen it before. An image flashed into her mind: Ram standing in front of her, the sleeve of his green jacket torn.

The same material now fluttered on the rowan tree.

He had hauled himself out of the grave, he had said. Maybe he had snatched at this tree, clawed at it. Here was where he had caught his sleeve. She could picture him now, desperately trying to find something to cling on to, his hand reaching up . . . reaching up for . . . the rowan tree.

She screamed. 'The grave's there, below the rowan tree. That's where she's buried.'

It only took a second for them to fly into action, DI Graham shouting orders. One of the men had already pushed his spade into the ground. 'The earth's definitely looser here.' He looked up at Shanti. 'She's right. This is a fresh grave.'

56

9.20 P.M.

They were running now, like rats leaving a sinking ship
– gathering up papers, documents, carrying computers.
So many of them looked familiar. Politicians, businessmen. But they wouldn't make it. The police, the fire
brigade, would arrive soon. And there would be a record
of everyone who was there. They would not escape.

No sign of the Dark Man, and as I hurried down the
stairs no one even noticed me. They were too busy
saving their own worthless skins.

I was invisible.

The front door lay open now, no Dobermanns bar-
ring my way. I ran out. The alarms were still ringing and
even now, somewhere in the far distance, I was sure I
could hear the wail of fire engines coming towards us.

I crossed the driveway to the grass and slumped to the
ground. All around me it seemed there was chaos, yet I
was in a silent world of my own, thinking. Did this mean
it was all over? I could stop running? Now I could find
home, and my mother . . . I could learn about my father.
Get my life back.

Just as Serena had said, memories were flooding in all the time – memories of happy times with my dad, going fishing with him . . .

Fishing with him. I could see us together. Me and my dad, laughing, talking. And then a dark shadow seemed to step in. Someone else was there.

The Dark Man. Why was he always there?

He stepped into the picture, smiling, laughing, showing me how to use a rod – how to flick my line so it snapped into the water. He'd been my dad's friend.

And he'd betrayed him.

Now I knew why I had always hated him, and feared him. I hated him with a vengeance.

He was one of the conspirators.

Had my dad pretended to be one of them too, to find out the truth? Had he pretended to be caught up in their evil? He had learnt about them, tried to tell someone, and no one had listened. And when he'd learnt about the London bomb, he felt he'd had no choice but to try to defuse it himself.

And the Dark Man, the man he thought was his friend, had let him take the blame for it and be turned into a monster.

I hadn't known any of this, just thought that my dad was one of them. That was why I had run after him that day – to stop him. That was the way it must have happened.

But everyone would know the truth now. I held on to that. They would know the truth about my dad. He was a hero. And that mattered more than anything else.

'Did you really think I would forget about you?'

195

His voice brought me out of my memories – the Dark Man, striding towards me.

'What's the point? It's over.' Why couldn't he see that? I called it to him, getting to my feet, glancing around for escape. I knew it would never be over for him though. He'd never give up.

He motioned with a click of his fingers and called out, 'The boy's here. Get him!'

Security guards seemed to appear from nowhere at his command.

His pace quickened into a run, and I was away too. This time I leapt the barbed wire, diving into a roll as soon as I was over it. I kept rolling down the hill into the woods until I was under the cover of the bushes and trees. Only then did I get to my feet and run, dodging between the trunks.

There was a shout to the left of me, one of the guards calling out, 'I see him!'

I dropped to the ground and started crawling. Now I could hear the dogs barking and howling. I stayed still for a moment and listened. The sounds seemed to be all around me. I heard the rustle of grass close by. It was too dangerous to stay where I was. I had no choice but to leap up again and run.

'There he is!'

They saw my movements in the darkness. I took a second to glance over my shoulder, almost didn't see the figure who suddenly swooped in front of me.

I only heard the click of the gun.

I stopped dead.

'Going somewhere?' It was one of the security guards,

menacing in black. He had his gun aimed at me.

'Stop him!' It was the Dark Man who called out, too close.

The guard's eyes flicked towards the sound of his voice, and I broke into a run. A heartbeat later he fired. I stumbled heavily, terrified by the sound, fell to the ground and tumbled down the hill. I rolled until I was hemmed in by bushes. I lay as still as I could, hardly breathing. His footsteps came so close I wondered how he could fail to see me lying there. A spider crawled over my hand. Still I didn't move, not a hair trembled on my head I was so still.

The guard stopped, feet from me. I could picture him standing there, looking all around him for the least movement, listening for the slightest sound.

I'm sure I heard it before he did: the snap of a twig. He thought it was me . . . and he fired again.

The sound made me jump. There was a cry from somewhere in the trees. The guard moved. Only then did I lift my head to watch him as he ran past.

I saw his body stiffen when he realised he hadn't shot me at all. I could hardly make out the figure on the ground because the guard was standing in front of it, but I could see that it didn't move, didn't stir. There was not a moan of pain. There was no sound at all.

The guard stepped aside. And I had a clear view of who was lying there.

It was the Dark Man.

I didn't wait to see any more, didn't waste a second. I was up and away.

And all the time I was thinking, *He's dead.*
At last. The Dark Man is dead.

57

They were digging frantically now. The earth was looser there, had been covered by overgrown turf so it would blend in with the rest of the graveyard. Even Dorothy was digging, down on her knees, grabbing handfuls of earth with her hands. Earth flew everywhere.

A spade hit something hard. They all stopped.

'A coffin!' DI Graham shouted. He threw the spade to one side and got on his knees, along with Dorothy, and began scraping soil away with his fingers.

They banged on the top of the coffin. If she was in there, if she was still alive, they wanted her to know help was on its way.

I hid in the woods for what seemed a long time, eventually creeping back up towards the drive. Through the trees I could see that people were still busy making their escape, carrying as much as they could take from the house. Cars were leaving, tyres skidding on the gravel as they hurried to get out of the estate before the police descended.

The plot was foiled.

I felt as if hours had passed, but I knew it was only minutes. As soon as the police arrived I would step out of the trees. I was shaking with the thought of it.

At last, to be able to tell someone who I was.

And then I saw him.

I thought at first I was imagining things – my nightmare come to haunt me again – because it couldn't be him. He was dead.

The Dark Man, holding his arm, stumbling out of the bushes towards one of the cars, making his escape.

He'll never die, I thought.

And now he was going to be off before anyone came. I could live with any of the others getting away, but not him. Never him.

I would not let him escape. Not after what he had done to my dad. Never. He had been after me for too long. Now it was my turn to be after the Dark Man.

He was already in the car as I ran towards the drive. I imagined myself leaping in through the window, or pulling open the door, struggling with him, stopping him.

That wasn't going to happen. His car was even now on the move. I had to follow him, but how? I looked around. There was a man struggling with a batch of papers, trying to open the door of his car. I made for him. Somehow I was going to make him follow the Dark Man. I pushed him into the seat just as he hauled the door open.

I took him by surprise. He tried to throw the papers at me. I scattered them around the car. But he wasn't finished. He leant over, fumbled to open the glove compartment. I saw at once what he was after. A gun.

He was an old guy, fifty maybe, and skinny with it. I had been through too much to let him beat me. I landed him a blow with my elbow and heard his jaw crack. He fell back. I was the one who reached the glove compartment first. I had the gun. I held it at his head, kept it steady on him as I slipped into the passenger seat. He did nothing to stop me. He was the one who was shaking, his eyes never leaving the gun in my hand.

'I've always wanted to say this,' I said. And somehow I knew it was true; I *had* always wanted to say this. I nodded to the Dark Man's car rolling smoothly down the drive. 'Follow that car.'

The man didn't move. He licked his lips nervously. 'You're only a boy. You don't know how to use that thing.'

He was wrong actually. As soon as I had the gun in my hand and my fingers closed around it, I knew I had held a gun before. And not just in a dream. I was the son of a soldier. My dad must have taught me. This was nothing new – but I didn't like the memory.

The man reached out for the gun. I aimed it out of the window of the car and fired. The sound exploded in the night air. Birds suddenly flocked from the bushes. The man gasped.

'Maybe you're right . . .' I said. 'Maybe I don't . . . So you'd better be careful or it just might go off again.'

58

9.35 P.M.

The protestors were still there on the main road, chanting, waving banners, shouting. Some of the police here had obviously been alerted about something. I saw a line of them trying to stop the cars as they turned right on to the road. They had no chance. Too few police, too many cars. And all trying to leave in a hurry. They didn't even notice the Dark Man's car as it left the drive and headed in the opposite direction. Why was he going back that way – towards Greenock and the river?

I motioned the man beside me to follow him. There was something very familiar about this man. I knew I had seen him before. But there was no time to think about that. The Dark Man was trying to escape. If I knew him, and I felt I did, he would have an escape plan in case anything went wrong. So what was down this way? A water festival. The river. Boats. Lots of boats. Who would notice one boat among many? A boat that would sail him down the river, where he could be picked up by another ship and head . . . anywhere in the world. New identity, new life.

Would they ever find him then?

No way. I was after him. I wasn't going to let him escape.

'Don't lose him,' I said.

The man ducked every time I waved the gun about wildly. If I hadn't had the gun, he would have tackled me for sure. But the gun gave me power. I hated the feel of it in my hand, but if it was going to take me to the Dark Man, I would hold it for as long as I needed it.

Would he know I was behind him? Surely not – even if he saw the car, he would just think it was just one of the other conspirators taking the same route.

There were other cars joining the road now, coming from some slip road where they had been diverted to avoid Hanover House. They were all heading for the festival. I didn't take my eyes from the Dark Man's car. It suddenly swerved dangerously. He was losing blood, wounded. Maybe even dying. I hoped so. I wanted him to die, but more than that I wanted him brought to justice.

We sped along the coast road, passed fire engines roaring toward Hanover House, police cars too, blue lights flashing. I glanced at the man beside me. His face was trembling as if he'd had some terrible shock.

'Did you really think you'd get away with it?' I asked him.

He turned to me then, for just a second. 'We would have . . . if it hadn't been for you.'

'Get it open!'

They prised the lid and Shanti's heart thumped. She

prayed they hadn't been too late, that Sapphire would still be alive.

The wood splintered and they clawed at the lid with their hands, pulled it apart.

Then every one of them fell back.

Sapphire Lennox lay there. She reminded Shanti of Snow White with her pale white skin and her black hair. She was even prettier in the flesh than she had looked in the photographs that were always splashed in all the papers.

She didn't stir, still as death.

'Is she dead?' Shanti murmured. She was sure she must be. No one so pale, so still, could possibly be alive. She turned to Angus Lennox. He had great tears in his eyes, standing there like a block of stone. He didn't look at Shanti, didn't take his gaze off his beloved daughter. His treasure.

'Inspector.' His voice trembled with rage. 'I have a very important phone call to make.'

59

The Dark Man kept glancing in the mirror. There were other cars on the road behind him now, but that one car had been with him since he'd left the house.

The boy.

Why was he so sure of it?

Because the boy wouldn't let go – relentless as death. The pain seared through his arm, and for a moment he lost control of the car. It veered on to the hard shoulder. He had to stay conscious. Not far to go. Already he could see the Big Wheel circling in the sky. *Keep your eyes on that*, he told himself. *Head for that. Soon be there. Then you can rest.*

To get to the waterfront he would have to pass through the fairground. He would have to leave his car at the entrance. There was no other choice. The fair was even busier now, the car park full. The Dark Man ignored the signs, determined to park as close to the entrance as he could. I could see his car weave its way through the queuing traffic, pushing in front of other cars. I heard horns blare at him angrily.

I would have to be careful not to lose him now. If I took my eyes off him in that crowd, in the dark, I might.

It was as if we were moving into another world. People were everywhere, laughing, enjoying themselves – families taking their children on a treat, couples out on a date, all of them unaware of the drama that was unfolding only a couple of miles away at Hanover House. The booming music of the fair and the squeals of delight grew louder as we reached the car park.

The man beside me twitched. 'His car's stopped. There.' He pointed to where the Dark Man's car was parked. The door hung open. I could see the Dark Man, only steps out of it, clutching his arm, making for the waterfront and escape.

'I'm not one of them, you know.' The man grabbed at my sleeve. And when he said that I remembered where I had heard that voice before: on a television broadcast – he was a presenter. He was famous, one of the most famous television presenters in the country. Of course, I thought, the Dark Men would want to get people from the media behind them too – people who could go on television and assure the public that order had been restored. People the public trusted for their integrity. Ha!

'Forced into it, were you?'

He nodded. 'Yes. Blackmail.' His voice shook. 'They blackmailed me.'

'Well, you'll be able to tell the world on television tomorrow all about it, then, won't you?'

'I will,' he said. 'I will.'

I looked into his eyes. *Liar*, I thought. He'd be off the second I was out of the car, racing through the night to get away.

I glanced back to make sure I could still see the Dark Man. I couldn't afford to lose sight of him. I stepped out of the car, moved back, keeping the door wide open. I could see the driver itching to make his getaway. The crowds were surging into the fairground. 'Hey!' I called to them. 'Look who's here!' I pointed into the car. 'Anybody want an autograph?'

His face fell. If he'd had the gun I would have been a dead man then. But *I* had the gun. I slipped it into a rubbish bin as an excited crowd rushed towards the car and swallowed it up. That would keep him busy for a while. I didn't want him getting away either. And I certainly didn't want him following me.

Then I was running. My eyes focused on the Dark Man again as he stumbled between the booths.

I wasn't going to lose him.

'Can I have a candyfloss, Barry?'

Barry's date, Michelle, was costing him a fortune. She'd already had a toffee apple, a couple of doughnuts and a hot dog. It was a good thing he hadn't had to pay for any of the rides, or he'd be skint by now.

'I don't know how you're keeping all this food down. You've been on every ride in this fair.'

Michelle blew a bubble. 'Constitution of an ox. I'm never sick. And anyway, I've not been on *every* ride.' Her eyes flew to the Ride of Death. 'Not been on that one.'

'It's broken,' Barry said, though he'd told her that about forty times already.

'The best ride in the fair – broken? It wasn't two days ago when my cousin was here. She said it was brilliant.'

'It is brilliant,' Barry assured her. 'And OK, it's not so much broken as . . . well, Uncle Ben, the man that owns the fair, he's too fussy. He's got this thing about safety. With me off he's not got enough people to work it. There's probably nothing wrong with it really.'

Barry pulled at her hand, leading her to the candyfloss stall. But just briefly, Michelle looked back.

The Ride of Death wasn't broken.

It was set in steel against the sky, begging her to come on it.

60

The Dark Man glanced back. He felt weak from the bleeding but he had to keep going. And the boy was behind him. Surely that was his figure, darting among the crowds.

He had hoped it was his imagination, but he knew it wasn't. The boy was real.

A family moved apart, a girl turned, and there he was, that dark hair tumbling over his forehead. And those eyes locked on him.

He had to shake him off.

The boy couldn't know exactly where he was headed, couldn't know that he had a boat waiting for him at the docks. No one knew that – his escape route in case things went wrong. And they had, thanks to the boy.

He turned away, began to hurry. *Forget the pain*, he told himself. He was used to pain. He had to lose the boy and it should be easy to lose him there, in that crowded fairground.

He'd seen me. *Let him*, I thought. Let him know I was after him. His face was white with pain. I had the upper hand. Nothing was going to stop me now.

I was suddenly surrounded by a group of clowns, blowing up balloons, honking horns. I had to dodge past them, was just in time to see the Dark Man leap on the Waltzers as they dipped and rose. I was right there after him. I jumped on to the revolving floor and edged round, searching for him. I was sure I saw him crouching at the far side.

'Hey, you!' One of the workers caught sight of me. He began to chase after me as I dodged between the spinning cars, swivelling them so that the passengers turned faster and faster. Some of them cheered me on, others tutted.

Where was the Dark Man? It was all I cared about.

I jumped from the revolving platform and there was no sign of him. I scanned the fairground as I took the steps down from the ride three at a time, saw him again. He was moving towards the carousel. He knew I was after him. His one quick look back at me confirmed that. Then he seemed to disappear between the leaping horses.

I was only seconds after him, tried to look through the horses as they moved up and down. Where had he gone from here? I lost him only for a moment. He was winding his way through the crowds again, trying to shake me off, trying not to lead me to his escape route.

61

Michelle had finished her candyfloss. She looked bored again. Barry was waiting for her to ask for something else to eat. He had begun to wonder how long she would keep that neat little figure of hers.

'So, want to go over and see the fireworks?' Barry suggested. 'They start soon.'

But Michelle wasn't listening. She was staring at the sign beside them.

KEEP OUT
DANGER

'We would see the fireworks great from up there.' She was looking up at the highest point on the Ride of Death.

He wished she would shut up about that. 'I told you it's broken.'

'You said it wasn't. You said it was only because it was your night off.'

That was true – and Barry hadn't been lying. He really did believe that. There was probably nothing wrong with the new roller coaster. He'd learnt how to operate it and it had been working just fine the other night. They'd made loads of money from it in the few days they'd been here. But Uncle Ben was a stickler for safety, and with this being Barry's night off, he was sure his boss had closed it because he didn't have enough staff to work the blinking thing. That was all. Hadn't he heard Uncle Ben moaning about just that this morning? Not enough staff to man the rides. Losing money.

'It's only because I'm off tonight,' he said, trying to impress her. 'There's no one else qualified to work it.'

And that, in a way, was the truth.

Michelle's eyes lit up. 'You mean, you could work it?'

'I'm a trained operator. Skilled.' He didn't add it was all computerised anyway. Then he realised what Michelle was thinking. 'I don't think that's a good idea, Michelle.'

'I thought you said you practically ran this place, you and this Uncle Ben guy.'

'That's true but . . .'

'But nothing.' Michelle pouted her lips. 'If I'm not going on the Ride of Death . . . I might as well go home.'

'Don't do that, Michelle.'

He didn't want her to go, not this early. It wouldn't be much of a date finishing before ten o'clock. He hadn't had time to make his move yet. Not even a snog. She'd been too busy scoffing her face.

Michelle slipped her arms round his neck. 'You wouldn't get fired or anything. You're the top guy around here.'

'No . . . no . . . I wouldn't get fired. Me? Can't do

without me around here.'

He was digging himself ever deeper and he knew it.

Michelle pulled at his sleeve. 'Come on, then . . . wait till I tell my pals I got a private go on the Ride of Death.'

62

10 P.M.

I saw him stumble again. He was slowing down. His bullet wound was holding him back. He'd never get away from me now. I began to run to catch up with him when, out of nowhere, a tumble of acrobats leapt in front of me.

'Come and see the Great Carolas!' they were calling.

And the crowd did. They gathered round them, cheering, as the Great Carolas began to jump on to each other's shoulders, building themselves into a pyramid. I tried to dodge round them but there were too many people, and more gathering every second to watch the show. And I was in the middle of them.

I stood on tiptoe, trying to see past the acrobats and the crowds, to watch where he was going.

And he was gone.

The Dark Man was gone. One minute I had a clear view of him, and the next . . . no sign at all. I blinked, stared. He had to be there. I couldn't have lost him. I wouldn't.

I didn't even think. I ducked under the pyramid.

There were shouts and yells. I caught someone's leg with my foot, nudged against an arm. I tried to apologise, wished I could explain that this was a life-or-death situation. I felt them all wobble as I pushed through them. The Great Carolas began to topple and roll to the ground.

Too many people. There were too many people. How could I hope to see one man among so many? I ran to the bridge that spanned the river and led from the fair to the waterfront. He had to cross there if he was making for a boat. It was crowded with people thronging from the fair to the docks for the fireworks. I stepped up on to the wall of the bridge so I could look out over the crowds. I had only lost sight of him for moments. Could he have made it this far? Over the bridge to the waterfront without me seeing him?

He had been slowing down, I told myself. He was wounded, dripping blood.

Dripping blood.

I retraced my steps. I checked the iron bridge, but there was not a trace of blood anywhere. Back I moved, and back, step by step. Somewhere I would find his trail.

I almost slammed into the high fence around the roller coaster. I stopped dead.

The Ride of Death was lying in darkness. I stared up at it. The track was laid out in a figure of eight, in the centre a corkscrew loop of spirals. What made it special was its height, the sharp turns on the track that loomed over the river and the heart-stopping vertical drops. There were two trains of cars. Both lay still now. One sat at the bottom on the far side of the track. The carriages on my side sat at the highest point, above the river, out of sight of the fair. Out of the way. Uncle Ben had thought it was too close to the edge of the dock. It wasn't safe. It wasn't to be used.

A good place to hide. I searched the ground around the fencing. Then I saw it, lying on a piece of white tarpaulin – a drop of blood like a dark ruby.

No one seemed to have noticed me. I was invisible. I slipped beneath the fence and hurried over to the carriages waiting on the far side.

I looked around. Was he lying somewhere in a shadowy corner of one of the cars? But each car was empty.

Keeping low, I hurried round to the back of the ride. I looked up at the other set of carriages sitting at the top of the roller coaster. I was sure I could see one of the cars sway, as if someone had moved inside it. Could he have climbed up so high, even in pain, hauling himself up? Yes, the Dark Man could do that. And another smudge of fresh blood on the frame confirmed it.

The Dark Man was up there.

I began to climb the Ride of Death.

63

10.05 P.M.

There was a shimmer of movement below. It brought him back on full alert. The Dark Man didn't have to look to see who it was.

Would he never give up? He had stopped the plot, cleared his father's name. Wasn't that enough for him? Yet, he was still here. The Dark Man peered over the edge of the car and could see the boy climbing the steel frame towards him. Here on the gloomy side of the fairground, where no one else could see him.

His heart was thudding. He had no energy to go any further.

Let him come, the Dark Man thought as the boy climbed closer. It was time to finish this for once and for all.

'We'll have to crawl under the fence, Michelle.' If Barry hoped that would put her off, he was disappointed.

'That just makes it more exciting.'

She crawled under like an expert, as if she'd been

doing it for years. 'This is just like that movie.'

'I hope you don't mean *Final Destination 3*?' Barry said, and she giggled.

'No, it was romantic movie. The hero sang a song. They were on the big wheel, I think. *Grease* or something.'

'Don't expect me to sing to you, Michelle.'

'You're that funny, Barry. I think you're just the coolest guy I've ever met.'

Barry had been about to stop her, to tell her it was no good, not worth taking the risk of Uncle Ben's wrath. But in that moment he was lost. *The coolest guy she'd ever met?*

He helped her into the first car, tightened up her harness.

She squeezed his hand. 'This is so exciting, Barry.'

He knew it was the wrong thing to do. He knew he was going to regret it. But he no longer cared. Michelle thought he was the coolest guy she'd ever met.

Barry headed for the start button.

Michelle was excited as she waited for Barry to jump into the carriage with her. She wanted to be up there on high, just the two of them, and see all the people like wee insects below her. She wanted to tell her mates all about it. This was going to be a ride to remember.

64

10.15 P.M.

I climbed higher and higher, finally reaching the top line of cars, and he was there, in one of them, waiting for me, ready for me. He held a gun in his unsteady hand, aimed directly at me. Why wasn't I afraid? Perhaps I hated him too much to be afraid. He was leaning back against the seat, his face pale. I could see the blood seeping through his suit. I felt no pity for him at all. I stepped from the frame into the first car – the car in front of him. I held tightly on to the safety harness to steady myself, and faced him.

'The end of the road.' His voice sounded unreal, rising above the sights and sounds from the fair below, the distant shouts and screams, the lights sparkling on the dark river. And I remembered another time, high in a lift shaft, with that same voice echoing across to me.

I had thought then that he was my father. Now I knew he wasn't. I had had a father, and the Dark Man had played a big part in his death. That was the reason I would never let him go.

The reason I hated him.

'The end of the road.' I echoed his words.

'You've done well. I knew you would. I always feared you would be our nemesis.'

'I don't need you to tell me that.' Did he think I would like his compliment? There was one more last thing I needed to know. 'Where's my mother?'

Surely I deserved to be told that.

He shook his head. 'Don't you think if I'd known that I would have used her to flush you out?' He drew in a deep breath. Was he dying? 'She's gone. Disappeared. Don't know where.'

Was that the truth? I'd find her, I promised myself. I'd be able to find her now – my dad's name cleared, me safe. Now she could step out of the shadows too.

'It's over,' he said. 'Let me go on my way. I have a boat waiting.' He nodded towards the docks. Somewhere out there, a boat would take him down the river that led to the sea, and from there to freedom – another country, another identity. He held out his free hand towards me, a hand covered with blood. 'I don't want to kill you. I never wanted to kill you. Don't you know that?'

I shrank back from him, confused. I didn't want him anywhere near me. I looked down. The river rippled below me. The sounds of the fair seemed to be coming from another distant world. I tried not to think about how high up we were. How far down the earth was. How deep that dark water.

'It's over . . . for you, for all the Dark Men.'

'You won't be able to stop everything,' he said.

'But they'll stop enough. It won't be worldwide. And it had to be everything or nothing for your plan to work.

So, for you, it is over.'

'There are too many of us,' he said. 'We'll rise again. Wait and see.'

'You'll try. But they'll know about you now. And there's more good people in the world than bad. Good people always win in the end.'

People are expendable, he had once said. But no one's expendable.

It was then the carriage began to shake. I stumbled, fell inside the car.

The Ride of Death began to move.

65

The carriages catapulted forward, moving faster and faster towards the first sharp turn. I manoeuvred myself into the seat of the car, wrapped my arms round the harness, held on tight. Behind me, I saw the Dark Man fumble for his harness too.

But this ride was broken, surely. I had seen the signs. It was still in darkness. Why was it moving?

'It's too late.'

Was that my voice? Or was it his?

'You'll never win.'

This time it was definitely me, calling across the night as the train of cars rushed forward. There would always be decent people standing up against the Dark Men of the world.

I knew it was true. It might take time, but good always triumphs over evil.

I caught my breath. The car was suddenly sent hurtling round a bend, so furiously I was sure it would come right off the track. I saw the river zoom towards us, then at the last second there was a heart-stopping turn and then another, and another. Then we suddenly came to a stop right at the top of the track, could go no higher.

But it only stopped for a moment, teasing us.

I had no time even to think. The track plunged in a spine-chilling drop. I could feel myself almost flying from the car. How I managed to hold on I don't know. I crouched down as deep as I could manage, clinging to the leather harness. I still felt the pull as the ride plummeted on its vertical course, heading for the corkscrew loops.

Uncle Ben came running through the crowds. He could see the Ride of Death, cloaked in darkness. Yet it was moving. He called out to one of the fairground workers at a nearby stall. 'Who started that ride?'

The boy was looking up in alarm. 'I don't know. There's signs everywhere. I never saw anybody, Uncle Ben.'

Ben pushed him away, pulled at the fencing. His eyes were scanning the carriages. He had hoped no one was in them. No such luck. Someone was up there, screaming, drunk probably, as the cars started to accelerate to the top again.

I was thrown forward, then back, as we spiralled into a corkscrew loop. The wind whipped my face. I felt my fingers slipping. If I lost my grip, I was done for.

Michelle was screaming. 'This is fantastic!'

'It's going too fast.' Barry was talking almost to himself.

'It's supposed to go fast,' Michelle assured him. Then her face fell. She turned to him. 'Isn't it?'

66

10.20 P.M.

As we hit the bottom I felt as if every bone in my body rattled and shook. This would be the time to leap out, run, as the train of cars slowed past the entrance gates. But by the time I pulled myself together, the ride had begun to rise again, faster this time.

I heard his cruel laugh behind me. 'Fun, eh?'

But his voice was weak.

JJ snapped his phone shut. All the way to Hanover House he had been trying to contact the boy again. A team of policemen had arrived before JJ, but there was no sign of the boy at the estate. Why hadn't he waited at the house? JJ was nearly there now. He hoped something hadn't happened to him, but he had a feeling that the boy was special; he could look after himself. There would be time enough to find him when this was all over.

Many top men had already been arrested at Hanover House, others apprehended trying to make their escape.

They would hunt down the rest.

In Downing Street, COBRA meetings were taking place; the police and the army were on full alert.

All over the world, governments had been alerted. The boy had done it.

In Tokyo the police had taken over the airport, rushing into the terminal building. They found bombs hidden and ready to be detonated on the runway – the same bombs that were found at Heathrow, Charles de Gaulle, JFK and all the other major airports in the world.

In Sydney they found bombs strategically placed under the Harbour Bridge, timed to go off at the exact same time as the bombs under Washington Bridge in New York and the Golden Gate Bridge in San Francisco.

Air Force One, just preparing for take-off, was held back and searched. One of the President's aides was found to have a suicide belt around him, packed with explosives.

The new Vice President, who'd been sitting in the Oval Office as if it was his already, was arrested.

And hidden deep in his computer files, there were lists of the members of the conspiracy and the sleeper cells all over the world.

67

The Ride of Death was vibrating. Barry didn't like the sound of it one bit. 'Something's wrong.'

Michelle snapped back at him. 'See if I die on this ride, Barry . . . we're finished!'

Was the ride swaying? No, had to be his imagination. And the sound . . . somewhere underneath the screams and shouts from the fairground . . . the sound of grinding metal coming loose. No, he was freaking himself out – it was all normal.

'I feel dizzy,' Michelle complained. And she vomited over the side.

Uncle Ben had to be careful how he stopped this thing. He could see the couple in one of the cars as it plummeted down. Oh no, surely that wasn't Barry up there! He checked out the other set of carriages. It was high up, heading for the top as this one came down.

Was anyone in that one? He peered into the darkness, thought there might be a movement, but when he stared there was nothing. No, he decided. It was just that daft Barry and his date, crammed into one car.

He had to make sure the ride stopped when they were near the bottom, and get them out quickly. He shouted to the other fair workers to get the crowds back to a safe distance.

The ride was lurching. He could hear the steel shuddering. It should have been dismantled today. They were supposed to come here and take it down! He could see the frame shake against the sky. No time to lose.

The ride roared us round a bend, and suddenly the carriage swung upside down. I'd be thrown clear for sure. I wrapped my arms tighter around the leather harness . . . and tried to keep my legs inside the car.

Yet, I suddenly wasn't afraid. *Enjoy the ride, Ram*, I thought. Because I had done it. Nothing could take that away from me. I had cleared my dad's name, and I had the Dark Man within my grasp. Soon I'd be able to step out from the shadows. I'd be a hero too, not just the boy with no name.

But, for now, I was a boy at the fair, and I was having a ball.

The cars began to accelerate to the top again. I could hear distant screams coming from the other carriage – not screams of enjoyment any more, but of real fear. In a second I knew why. The Ride of Death was breaking up. It was coming apart.

Michelle tried to stand up. It was Barry who pulled her down. He pointed to where Uncle Ben stood on the ground, waving his arms about madly. 'Look, they're trying to stop it.'

'It's going to come off the tracks!' Michelle was panicking. She had loosened the harness, had one leg over the car. 'We've got to get out of here. Now!'

'We've only got one chance,' Barry yelled at her. 'When it gets to the bottom, we jump.'

Barry could see Uncle Ben and the other men running, calling, warning them to be ready. They knew the car was about to fly from the tracks. The car slowed; they were still high up, but closer to the ground. Their last chance.

Uncle Ben shouted, 'Jump!'

Barry grabbed Michelle. He didn't have to be told twice.

68

10.25 P.M.

The carriage had reached the top again. It came to a sudden halt. The steel was shuddering all around me. I slipped out of the harness. Now was my chance to climb down to safety. I turned to look at the Dark Man. The gun was gone from his hand. The time for guns was over. He was so close I could have reached out and touched him. But neither of us moved.

'So how's that memory of yours doing now? Has the ride shaken out a few of the missing pieces?' he rasped.

'I've cleared my dad's name. That was what I wanted most of all. I cleared his name! I remember I ran after him that day to stop him planting that bomb. But he wasn't planting it . . . he was trying to defuse it. That's why I needed you to shout that out. I wanted them to know the truth. I've remembered it all. Now everyone will know he wasn't a villain. He was a hero. My dad was a hero.'

Why was he saying nothing? He knew I had won. Was that what was bothering him? Because I had beaten him? Me? Just a boy.

'You *think* you've remembered everything.' His face had half disappeared into the darkness, underlit by a green glow from the fair below. He seemed to fill the black silence with his words.

The Ride of Death was trembling. There was no time to waste. I gripped the edge of the car to steady myself. I should have been climbing down, calling for help. But I had to find out what he meant.

'There is nothing else. It's over. Why can't you just accept it? They'll come for you, they will. Now they know who you are. They'll all be after you. The Dark Men because you betrayed them, and the law. It'll never be over for you.'

'Why couldn't you just let me go?'

I had a simple answer to that. 'Because of what you did to my dad.'

'I would have disappeared and you'd never have needed to know the truth.'

The frame jerked and I almost toppled.

'What do you mean "the truth"? I know the truth.'

'It will never be over for you either,' was all his reply.

He was trying to frighten me, and he was succeeding. 'It is over for me,' I said. 'I'll find my mother. The authorities will find her. I'll get my life back.'

'Haven't you worked it out yet?'

'Worked out what?' I screamed it at him. 'I've worked everything out! I know everything!'

At that moment the sky lit up with fireworks. Catherine wheels and rockets and sprays of gold and green and blue and red. I could hear the cheers from the crowds on the other side of the dock, the gasps of delight. And the Dark Man's voice as hard as the punch of a fist.

'Of course you weren't trying to stop your dad from planting the bomb . . .' He seemed to delight in the silence, in the pause before he spoke again. 'He was trying to stop *you* . . .

'You were the Lone Bomber.'

69

The world swam around me. The sky spun. I clamped my hands over my ears to block out everything he was saying. He was a liar. He always lied.

Yet I knew as soon as he spoke the words that it was the truth.

I was the Lone Bomber.

And now I had to remember, couldn't stop the memories flooding back.

I had been planting the bomb that day.

I had turned from my dad long before, ashamed of him and what he had become. I had found another hero – the Dark Man. I had wanted the Dark Man to be my father. He was my dad's friend, still a soldier, someone to look up to. I had wanted to be like him. He had taught me to shoot, talked about a world where people like us would rule, the best from all races. And the rest . . . were expendable.

And I had believed him. I had been the one drawn to the Dark Man and his ideas, not my dad. I had hung on his every word.

'You were the son I wanted. You came with me every-where. You wanted to.'

232

And he was right. He had taken me to Hanover House. That was why I recognised it. That was the memory I'd had of listening behind the door. And I had overheard their plans. Every detail.

My dad hadn't told me anything that day in the dark tunnel. I had known it all along.

It was as if the Dark Man could read my mind, knew what I was thinking.

'But you learnt too much that day at Hanover House. You heard every secret we had, every detail of Operation Ram. Secrets given out to only a few.'

I recalled, too, being stunned by their plans, amazed at their audacity.

'They wanted you dead. Do you remember that? You were too dangerous.'

And now, finally, I was remembering everything I didn't want to remember. It was the Dark Man who had protected me that day. I had walked towards them and with his hand on my shoulder I had felt safe. I wanted to please him. I had always wanted to please him. They thought I was too dangerous to be left alive. I knew I wanted to do something to make him proud. It was me who had suggested I plant that first bomb.

They'll never suspect a boy. Let me prove myself. My own words came back to me then, in a voice that didn't tremble with fear. It was bold and cold as ice, like the Dark Man's. Because I remembered now that I had wanted so much to be one of them. The Dark Man had been my hero, the man I wished was my father. I wanted to make him proud. *They have boy soldiers all over the world. Let me be one of them*, I had said.

And they had. Because then I would be tied to them for ever. The Dark Man had shown me where to plant the bomb, how to escape, how to be safe. He hadn't reckoned on my dad.

'At first we thought you'd been killed by your own bomb.' The Dark Man's voice cut through my memories. 'When we knew you hadn't died in the blast, we couldn't understand where you'd gone. But we didn't want anyone else to find you, or find out about you. So we got rid of any witnesses who had seen you and we kept looking out for a boy on the run. When I found you those weeks ago, I couldn't believe you had survived, couldn't understand what had happened – till I discovered you'd lost your memory. That explained almost everything.'

No, no, no. I wouldn't listen, but I had to.

'I never wanted you dead. I wanted you back, the way you were.'

The way I was – arrogant and superior and . . . like the Dark Man.

'That's why *I* came after you,' he said. 'No one else. You were my recruit, the son I wanted. You were a Dark Man in waiting. You still are.'

NO!!!! I tried to shake the memory out of my head, make it false. But I couldn't.

My dad had followed *me* that day . . . not the other way around. He knew what I planned to do and he had tried to stop *me*. And there, in that underground tunnel, I saw what I had become reflected in my dad's eyes.

Yet my dad had still blamed himself. '*It's all my fault,*' he had told me. '*I was falling apart, couldn't see what I was doing to you . . . what he was doing to you.*' And he meant the Dark Man. I knew then who the figure I had seen with the Dark Man was, the one who frightened me even more than him.

That figure was me.

'*But it's not too late,*' my dad had said. '*I can stop this bomb going off. We can go together to the authorities, tell them everything. You know, don't you? You can stop it.*'

And in the dark of that cold, damp car park, I had come back. I was me again. Not the boy I had become. Not the follower of the Dark Man.

He had run off to defuse the bomb, and I had run out into the open air to wait for him. But he had been too late . . . by seconds.

I was outside when the bomb went off, outside in the cold February air. And I knew immediately my dad was dead. And I had killed him. I didn't know how to handle it.

It hadn't been the blast that had made me lose my memory. It had been my own guilt and shock. I'd hated what I had become: the selfish, arrogant, self-centred boy who thought he was better than everyone else; who thought people were expendable; who admired the Dark Man and all the Dark Men of the world. I had hated that other self so much that I had killed him that day.

On the day my father died, the old me died with him.

Without knowing it, I had given myself a second chance. A fresh start. And I realised . . . I liked the me I had become.

I had lost my memory . . . and found my conscience.

'So now you remember,' said the Dark Man,

examining my face with satisfaction. His words bit into my heart. 'Now you know you're ours for ever.'

'No!' I screamed it out. I wouldn't be theirs. I'd rather die.

The train of cars began to tremble. Steel broke from steel. I could hear screams from below, see people rushing further back to safety.

The Ride of Death was falling apart, staggering on its long steel legs, falling towards the deep, dark river.

I didn't take my eyes off his. I knew it was collapsing. I didn't care. I had won and he knew it.

But, in a way, he had won too.

It was done.

I didn't want to live – not knowing what I did now.

I spread my arms wide as if I could fly . . . and I prayed.

70

MONDAY

Shanti arrived back after midnight to find the fairground in chaos. Uncle Ben didn't even know she'd been gone. He'd find out soon enough when the police – and the press – descended on them in the morning.

She called to one of the fairground workers hurrying past her. 'What happened?'

'That idiot Barry started up the Ride of Death and it collapsed. Nobody's been hurt. Don't worry. Barry is in real trouble now. Chance in a million no one was killed.' And he hurried off to help Uncle Ben.

Shanti went inside the caravan. She peeked into the bedroom. Aunt Serena was still sleeping, breathing deeply and evenly. Shanti wanted to shake her, tell her all that had happened, ask her now to tell her about her past. She was too excited to sleep.

They had saved Sapphire Lennox's life.

She'd been given just enough oxygen to last till noon the next day and the doctor had managed to revive her. Thank the Lord, Shanti thought, that she had been drugged and unconscious the whole time. She would have no memory of her ordeal. Her father (had Shanti ever seen a man so angry?) had told the authorities everything about the plot and his involvement in it. He had been one of their top men, but in the last days he'd had a change of heart, wanted no part of the plan, wanted to warn the world. And this was the Dark Men's way of shutting him up.

But the authorities already knew about the plot. Ram had done it.

And now it was Shanti who was being given the credit for saving Sapphire. She was still sure she didn't have the gift, but she had something. Ram hadn't told her about catching his sleeve on the tree. She had used her observation, her common sense to figure that out. Maybe that was as much of a gift as anything else. She wanted to ask her aunt if that was so. She wanted to ask someone.

But there was no one to talk to. She couldn't bear to disturb her aunt.

So she took her place beside her aunt's bed and held her hand, and wondered where Ram was.

JJ was beside Jane's bed when she woke up in the early hours of the next morning. He was exactly who she wanted to see. She'd been dreaming about him – dreaming of his severe face, his kind eyes. Nice dreams.

'Everything OK?' she said softly.

'Everything's wonderful,' he said, and he meant it.

He turned on the television in the corner for the breakfast news bulletin. The main news was that an international plot had been averted during the night in a series of raids. There was film of raids at foreign airports, of people being arrested, of troops surrounding government buildings both here and abroad.

'*Police are saying that the scale of the attack, codenamed Operation Ram, would have changed the face of the world had it been successful. It has also emerged that Angus Lennox, the politician whose kidnapped daughter was rescued last night after a tip-off, had vital information about the plot. Sapphire Lennox is recovering in hospital after being buried alive in a graveyard outside Edinburgh.*'

There was footage of an overjoyed but exhausted-looking Angus Lennox standing outside an emergency department. Reporters clustered around him, pushing microphones in his face. He was barely able to speak through his tears.

'I have disclosed vital information about Operation Ram to the Prime Minister and the security services. I couldn't speak until I knew my daughter was safe.'

'I'm so glad,' Jane said. 'I never did think it was a publicity stunt.'

'And it's all down to one boy,' JJ said softly.

'One boy?' she asked.

He patted her hand. 'I'll tell you about it later.'

She let his hand rest on hers and she smiled. It was probably only a coincidence, but she had told the police on the day of the London bombing about a boy. She had seen him that day, after the blast. A running boy, distraught, crying. Such a little thing, but she could never understand why no one had wanted to know who he was.

Gaby and Zoe had had a sleepover and saw the news together.

'That has to be our Ram. That was his secret. Operation Ram,' Zoe said.

'What do you mean, "our Ram". He was *my* Ram. I met him first.'

'Your Ram, my Ram. Does it matter? He's saved the world!'

'Do you think we should tell the cops?' Gaby was already picturing interviews, model assignments, lucrative book deals.

'You've got to be joking, Gaby. Nobody believes a word you say. You've got us into enough trouble. Better just forget it. If Ram wants us to talk about it, I'm sure he'll let us know.' Zoe was remembering she was the one who got the valentine.

'Anyway,' Gaby went on, losing interest. 'Are you going to let me pluck your eyebrows or not? I need practice if I'm going to be a beauty consultant.'

Faisal was on the phone to Kirsten first thing. 'Have you heard the news today, Kirsten?'

'Is that you, Faisal? You've just woken me up! What news?'

'Operation Ram! His name did mean something. He stopped the plot, Kirsten, and we helped him.'

Kirsten was proud too. 'We can't tell anybody about him, Faisal, you know that.'

'I know . . .' Faisal sighed. Of course he knew it. Because telling anyone about Ram would mean telling the whole story about Noel, and maybe Paul as well. Too many questions. 'I know . . . but it would be so great to get some recognition. We do all these wonderful things and can't tell a soul about them.'

'That's all you want, isn't it, Faisal? Everybody to know you're a hero!'

'Shut up, Kirsten!' he said. And he hung up on her.

Catman was getting ready to meet his family again. Shaved and dressed, he looked better than he had done in years. He had to do something about those teeth, though, he was thinking, when he heard the news on the radio.

The boy had done it. Operation Ram had been foiled because of him. Not that he'd ever doubted him. Not once. That boy was special.

Ryan didn't hear the news. He only knew the plot had failed in the middle of the night when his mother had roused him, and they both raced in secret to a ferry terminal and boarded a boat heading for the continent.

The plan had failed. His dad was gone. All Ram's fault.

One day, Ryan thought, *I am going to make him pay*.

Shanti saw the story, too, on the early morning news. Ram had done it. Now he could come out of the shadows. Funny there was no mention of any boy being involved, though.

Uncle Ben came into the caravan. He looked tired, drawn. He hadn't been to bed all night because of the collapse of the roller coaster.

'I'm sorry, Uncle Ben,' she said.

For once, he spoke to her softly. 'It wasn't your fault.' He sighed. 'Wasn't mine either. The police said I'd taken every precaution. It's the people who erected it who are in trouble, and stupid Barry, of course.'

He crossed the room, looked in on Serena. 'She's sleeping,' he said, as if Shanti didn't know it. Shanti didn't say her aunt was sleeping so soundly she wondered if she would ever wake up. She didn't have to. Uncle Ben knew.

He sat on a chair and all at once his face looked old and lined. 'What am I going to do without her, Shanti? I can't bear to think about it.'

He put his head in his hands, and for a moment she thought he was crying. But he wasn't. She went over and knelt in front of him. 'I'll help you, Uncle Ben.'

He looked at her and his smile was painful. 'I know you will.' He reached out and took her hand. 'We'll help each other.'

One day, maybe, her uncle would tell her where she came from, but not today.

EPILOGUE

How did I survive? I didn't want to. I did nothing to save myself as I plummeted towards the river, out of that cage of steel.

Down I plunged, deep into the water, giant arms of steel splashing around me, and all I could think of was that I had beaten the Dark Man. I had stopped the attack. I had kept out of his clutches till the end. And this was the final escape. I would die and be rid of him for ever.

Yet I had lived, my instinct for self-preservation greater than anything else. It had dragged me by the neck, hauled me out of the water, forced me to breathe again. I clambered out of the river some way down-stream, well out of sight of the crowds rushing to the edge of the dock where the Ride of Death had collapsed. I sat, shivering, and looked across the water for signs of the Dark Man, waited for him to emerge from the water after me. But he never did.

Had he survived?

I imagine that he did. Even wounded and bleeding. I

imagine that we are destined to be trapped together for eternity.

I walked till it was light, found a brazier under a bridge, where men were huddling to keep warm – early morning workers at the waterfront. They were listening to a news report on a radio and chatting. I rubbed my hands and held them towards the heat. Then I froze when I realised the men were talking about the Lone Bomber.

'They're saying now that he was actually trying to defuse the London bomb that day. Poor guy gets blown up trying to save lives and they turn him into a blinking villain.'

'It's no surprise to me,' another man said. 'The guy'd won medals and everything for bravery. He wouldn't have done a cowardly thing like blowing up innocent people.'

My dad, his name cleared. A hero again. Everything I wanted. I tuned into the end of the news report as the headlines were repeated.

'Politician Angus Lennox's daughter has been rescued. Her kidnapping has been linked to the international terrorist plot which was averted during the night.'

Shanti had done it.

I hugged at my arms, amazed I had any clothes left after that plunge. My jacket was in pieces after all I'd been through. I remembered then how my jacket had been caught on the tree above the grave . . . I'd forgotten to tell Shanti about that. Come to think of it, I hadn't even told her about the tree. A funny-looking tree – couldn't think what kind it was. Never mind.

Shanti hadn't needed that information. Shanti had done it anyway.

One of the men turned his radio off.

'A worldwide terrorist attack? Sounds a bit far-fetched. Bet the conspiracy theory junkies will be rubbing their hands in glee.'

'Aye. I reckon this government's just trying to score a few votes at the next election. Funny there hasn't been any bombs going off this morning, eh?'

The man looked at me, saw me smiling. 'What's so funny, son?'

'Well, maybe it's all true.'

He patted my shoulder. 'Wait till you're older – you'll understand. Don't believe everything you hear on the news.'

And I wouldn't. Because only I knew the truth, and the truth was more painful than anything else. How could I live with what I had done?

Yet there had to be a reason I had survived.

I'd make it up to my dad. I'd be the son he deserved. I'd help people. I'd seek out the Dark Men everywhere.

And one day, maybe, I would find my mother, and I'd be able to face her and not be ashamed any more.

My poor mother. I had vague memories now of her leaving my dad long ago. I had refused to go with her, pretending I wanted to stay with my dad, look after him. But it was the Dark Man I had wanted to stay with. And she knew that. She had also known what I'd planned to do that day, knew that my dad had tried to stop me. But how could she speak up? Tell the world her husband wasn't the Lone Bomber, but her son was?

What choice had she but to keep quiet?

I began to walk away.

One of the men called after me. 'Hey, where are you going, son? Stay here in the warm.'

'I've got to go,' I said.

The man fished in his pocket, drew out some coins, held them out to me. 'Here, get yourself something to eat.'

I thanked him, took the money. Good people, decent people. They were everywhere, no matter what the Dark Man thought.

I passed someone from the Salvation Army on the road, holding out a tin for the homeless. I took out some coins and dropped them in. I owed a shopkeeper money for a newspaper. This was the best I could do to pay him back. I wasn't going to begin my new life by not paying my debts.

And my name?

I have a name, same name as my dad. But I don't deserve to use it. From now on I'll just be Ram.

Maybe one day I'll earn the right to take back my name again.

I walked on. Back into the shadows.